MOTHER,

PLEASE DON'T DIE

by

Lurlene McDaniel

DARBY CREEK PUBLISHING

A Scholastic Book Fairs Edition

To Leslie's memory and for Claire Ellen and Julie.

*Special appreciation to Darcy Crowe for her help with
the medical aspects of this book.*

Cataloging-in-Publication

McDaniel, Lurlene.
Mother, please don't die / by Lurlene McDaniel.
    p. ; cm.
ISBN-13: 978-1-58196-028-X trade paperback
ISBN-13: 978-1-58196-072-3 Scholastic Book Fairs Edition
Summary: Thirteen-year-old tomboy Megan McCaffery is just beginning to enjoy growing up
when her mother is diagnosed with a cancerous brain tumor. Suddenly, Megan's life is turned
upside down, her hurt and anger coming between her and everyone she cares about, until she
realizes what her real priorities are.
1. Mothers and daughters—Juvenile fiction. 2. Teenagers—Juvenile fiction. 3. Cancer—
Patients—Juvenile fiction. 4. Terminally ill—Juvenile fiction. 5. Teenagers and death—
Juvenile fiction. [1. Mothers and daughters—Fiction. 2. Teenagers—Fiction. 3. Cancer—
Fiction. 4. Terminally ill—Fiction. 5. Teenagers and death—Fiction.] I. Title.
PZ7.M4784172 Mo 2005
[Fic] dc22
OCLC: 57347156

Published for Scholastic Book Fairs by Darby Creek Publishing
7858 Industrial Parkway
Plain City, OH 43064
www.darbycreekpublishing.com

Printed in the United States of America

2 4 6 8 10 9 7 5 3 1

978-1-58196-072-3

One

Megan Sue McCaffery ran into the kitchen of her house and let the screen door slam behind her. She skidded across the kitchen floor and tossed her dusty baseball glove on top of the counter. "We won," she announced to her sister, Audrey, who was scraping vegetables at the sink. "I hit a homer in the sixth and it drove in two runs. It's only two weeks into the school year, and already we've got the best softball team in Charleston! Wait until spring when we start playing seriously. Nobody will be able to beat us. What's for supper? And where's Mom?"

Audrey tossed her strawberry curls and glared at Megan. "Can't you do anything quietly? And get that filthy mitt off the counter! I declare, Megan, when are you going to start acting your age? You're thirteen, and you're still grubbing around on a baseball lot like a sand rat!" Audrey wrinkled her nose in disgust.

Megan sneered at her. Then she jerked open the

refrigerator and fished out an apple. *Funny how Audrey's Southern accent gets even thicker and stickier when she's mad,* Megan thought. "Shows what you know," Megan said as she grabbed the glove and jammed it under her arm. "It's a fielder's glove. Only catchers use a mitt."

"Well, excuse me!" Audrey put her hands on her hips. "I forgot the difference."

"And there's nothing wrong with baseball, either," Megan continued. "At least it's more interesting than talking on the phone with Rosemary all the time about getting married."

"Well, you just better take some lessons, little sister. If you don't get your act together, no boy is ever going to date you, much less ask you to marry him."

Megan bit down on the apple. The taste of the juicy fruit muffled her hateful reply to her sister.

"And don't spoil your supper. I'm fixing fried chicken like Mom does."

"Where is Mom?" Megan asked again.

Audrey gestured toward the door that led to the rest of the sprawling house. "She's got another one of her headaches. So that's reason number two that you don't need to come flying through the place like a kite with its tail on fire."

4

Immediately, a frown creased Megan's face and her squabble with Audrey was forgotten. "Another one? Poor Mom. That's the third one this week. I think they're getting worse."

"I think so, too."

"When's Dad coming home?"

"He had to take a last-minute deposition for court tomorrow, so he'll be here about seven. I told Thad to be home from Billy's by six-thirty."

Megan chewed on her lip, thinking about her mother's headaches. "Maybe I'll just peek in on her …"

"Not like that, you won't!" her older sister commanded.

Megan glanced down at her sweat-streaked, dirt-caked clothes.

"You just march yourself right up to our bathroom," Audrey continued, "and get a hot bath before you bother Mom. And put on something besides jeans. Dress like a girl for a change. When you're a bridesmaid in my wedding, you'll have to wear a dress that goes all the way to the floor."

"There's nothing wrong with girls in jeans," Megan grumbled, hoping to turn the discussion from Audrey's favorite topic—her wedding.

"Well, you don't look like a girl to me, Megan McCaffery."

Megan made a face at her sister. Then she darted through the swinging white door of the kitchen and scampered up the winding staircase to the bathroom she shared with Audrey. At least there was one good thing about Audrey getting married—Megan would finally have the bathroom that joined their separate bedrooms all to herself. She jerked Audrey's pantyhose from the shower bar and flung them into a corner. They fell next to her sister's silk blouse and linen skirt. Apparently Audrey had thrown them there when she'd come home from her job as a receptionist at a downtown Charleston travel agency. Living with Audrey was like living in a messy closet!

"Look at that," Megan muttered to her reflection in the mirror. "Audrey just lets stuff fall all over and then gripes at me about a baseball glove!" Megan pulled off her baseball cap, and her silky-fine brown hair fell to her shoulders in a tangle. She studied her dirt-smudged face, accented by sky blue eyes, a turned-up nose, and a pointed chin.

Megan took off her soiled clothes and stuffed them in the hamper. Then she filled the tub with warm water. She opened Audrey's prized bottle of bath oil, the one Brent, Audrey's fiancé, had given her for her birthday. Megan dumped a generous amount under the flowing tap. The air was filled with the sweet, flowery aroma. Megan lowered herself into the scented water and sighed contentedly.

She shampooed her hair and washed off the dirt from the baseball game. An angry bruise swelled on her right knee. She was injured when she slid into second base just as the opposing shortstop rushed over to tag her out. He missed her by a mile, but because he didn't like being beaten by a girl, he hit her hard, knocking the wind out of her and causing her to bruise her knee. But she got even with him. Smugly, she recalled chasing him down with a ball and coming up under his chin with her elbow. It wasn't very nice, but he didn't bother her for the remainder of the game.

After she bathed, Megan blew her hair dry, watching her body in the mirror. She was changing and she hated it. Megan had always been slim, tall, and athletic. She could outrun and out-hit any boy in her elementary school—and for that matter in her junior high, too. Then, this past summer, her body had started filling out, turning graceful and feminine.

She was still a fast runner, and she could still hit the ball a good distance. But she was suddenly no longer the best. It made her mad! What if she turned into another Audrey, all flowery and fluttery with nothing on her mind but boys and getting married? Megan shuddered just thinking about it.

Megan gathered the silky wisps of her shoulder-length hair into a rubber band. She dressed quickly in clean jeans and a light blue blouse and hurried down to her mother's bedroom. She rapped lightly on the door until she heard a muffled, "Come in." Megan slipped quietly into the room. The curtains were closed against the long, slanting rays of the descending afternoon sun. Her eyes adjusted to the dimness as she crossed to the giant four-poster bed where her mother was lying.

"Hey, Mom," Megan whispered in the dark. "How are you feeling?"

"Not good, honey."

"Did you take some aspirin?"

"Yes, but my head still hurts."

Even in the shadows Megan could see the pinched corners of her mother's mouth, the closed eyelids, and the deep, dark circles under her eyes. Megan gently eased herself onto the bed and lifted her mother's hand in hers. "Could I get you a wet cloth for your forehead?"

"Yes, thank you."

Megan got the washcloth and then resettled herself on the bed, hooking her bare heels on the bed frame and leaning one shoulder against a dark oak post. "We won our game, Mom."

"That's nice. I wish I could have been there. But I started getting sick around noon. When Audrey got in from work, I asked her to cook supper. You should help your sister." Adele McCaffery's voice was a strained whisper, and Megan had to tip her head downward to catch all of the words.

"She's doing just fine without me. It's no fun helping Audrey, anyway. She's so bossy. And all she ever talks about is her wedding!"

Mrs. McCaffery squeezed Megan's hand slightly. "Someday it will be your wedding, Megan. Then you'll understand what all the fuss is about."

"I'll never act like that," Megan insisted. Then she sucked in her breath. She was sorry she had bothered her mother with her feelings about Audrey. Megan changed the subject. "Would you like me to read to you, Mom?"

"That would be nice," Mrs. McCaffery said, her words barely audible.

Megan lifted a book from the nightstand and squinted at the print. She read to her mother until the quiet droning of her voice blended with the relaxed breathing of her mother. *She's asleep,* Megan realized. Megan closed the book and studied her mother's still form. She was terribly afraid for her mother. The headaches were sapping all of her energy, and no medication seemed to help.

Megan heard Thad tear through the front door downstairs and Audrey scold him to be quiet. Megan decided she'd better go down to help Audrey. After all, her mother had asked her to.

Megan rose from the bed and paused at the doorway. She looked at her mother with a lingering gaze of concern. *What is happening to you, Mom?* Megan silently asked. She walked down the stairs, the unanswered question whirling in her mind.

Two

"Hey, Megan! Wait up. Where are you headed in such a hurry?"

The sound of the male voice in the school hall behind Megan caused her to pause. She squared her shoulders and turned to face the coal black eyes of John-Paul Harrison, her next-door neighbor. He'd been her friend since first grade, but recently he seemed to have become a stranger.

"Hi, John-Paul. I was just heading for gym class."

"Well, wait up and I'll walk with you."

Megan was kind of uncomfortable around John-Paul these days. He'd changed. In June he'd gone off to summer camp and returned completely different from the boy she'd known for seven years. John-Paul had shot up, grown four inches. Now Megan could no longer look him in the eye without tipping her head backward. And he was no longer a scrawny kid. He'd developed a broad chest and muscular arms. The sun had darkened his already-brown skin. His

11

hair had grown longer, jet-black and straight, making him look even more like the native Iroquois of his ancestry.

The two of them walked down the hall in silence, threading their way through groups of kids. Silence stretched between them like a wire. Megan swallowed hard, hating how awkward she felt with John-Paul. She thought about the days when they'd run and played together as kids. They'd arm-wrestled and knocked cans off fence posts with slingshots. They'd caught fireflies in jars and set up a lemonade stand at the corner of their block.

John-Paul finally spoke. "Rosemary says she's going with Audrey up to the Citadel on Saturday to double-date with Brent and one of Brent's cadet buddies. I feel sorry for the guy, stuck with my sister for the whole night."

Megan appreciated John-Paul's effort to talk about a common topic. For years they'd both complained about their older sisters. Rosemary and Audrey had always been best friends, so Megan and John-Paul never lacked for stories to share. "Yeah. I can see the headlines now: 'Cadets Die of Boredom As Dates Talk Their Ears Off,'" she said, laughing.

John-Paul laughed, too. "Hey, I heard you hit a homer yesterday and saved the game for your team."

She blushed and was surprised by her reaction. "They weren't so tough. Where were you anyway? I didn't see you in the stands."

"I had a city league baseball game of my own. Did the other team give you any grief?"

Megan knew that John-Paul was aware of her reputation for being feisty on the field. It sort of embarrassed her. She confessed, "I had to take out the wise-guy shortstop in the third inning—but we won."

"Megan! Are you still fighting?" John-Paul teased.

"I don't like being shoved around by anyone, especially some smart-aleck boy who thinks that just because I'm a girl he can run all over me."

John-Paul stopped in front of the gym doors and looked at her, his black eyes twinkling with amusement. "It bugs you that us guys are catching up with you, doesn't it, Megan McCaffery?"

She lifted her chin defiantly. "I bet I can still outrun you, John-Paul Harrison."

"Only if I give you a head-start."

"Just name the time and place," Megan said.

He shook his head. "You just wait, Megan Sue."

13

Megan edged past him and pushed open the gym doors. The sound of his laughter made it impossible for her to speak.

"You'd better watch that temper!" he called as the doors slammed shut in his face.

Megan stomped into the locker room and jerked her locker open. She tried to calm down while she was changing for the outdoor playing field.

"Whew! You look meaner than a junkyard dog," Delsey Gartner said as she sat down next to Megan.

Megan gave Delsey an irritated glance. Megan liked the athletic Delsey. In fact, Delsey was one of the few girls Megan had ever liked. "Bad day," Megan answered through clenched teeth.

"Then I guess you won't be interested in what I just heard in the cafeteria."

Megan was curious. "I might be. What's it about?"

"A certain Becky Thorndyke and John-Paul Harrison."

"John-Paul Harrison is a toad. And words just cannot express what I think of Becky Thorndyke." The truth was, Megan didn't like Becky one bit and never had. Becky didn't walk; she *flounced*. She didn't speak; she *gushed*. Boys acted stupid around Becky. Megan remembered all of the Valentines Becky got

14

each year, each one signed by "Your secret admirer." Becky always ripped open the cards, giggled, and said, "Why, who in the world … ?" in her thick, Southern drawl. Becky Thorndyke made Megan even madder than Audrey did.

"Then I guess I'll keep it to myself … ," Delsey taunted.

"Oh, go ahead and spill it, Delsey, before you have a fit."

Glancing left and right, Delsey leaned forward, bracing her hands on the bench where Megan sat changing her gym shoes. "Guess who was kissing behind the baseball dugout down at the city park yesterday?"

Megan paused in the middle of tying her shoelaces. Her mouth flapped open and she gaped at Delsey. "You don't mean John-Paul and Becky were … were …" She couldn't get the words out. She kept seeing the darkly pretty Becky with her arms around John-Paul's neck, kissing him. "That's disgusting!" Megan stood up abruptly.

"What's the big deal? John-Paul's changed a lot this summer. He was always cute, but now he's gorgeous."

"Well, I hope John-Paul's had his rabies shots. I thought he had better sense. Just goes to show you what *I* know." Megan snatched up her street shoes and crammed them into her locker. "We're going to be late, and you know how mad Miss Dadey gets if you miss roll call."

Delsey scrambled to stand up and jogged with Megan out into the hot, South Carolina sunshine. "I didn't think you'd get so upset about it," she grumbled.

"I'm not upset about it."

Delsey slowed her pace, and Megan matched it as they joined their gym class on the playing field. "Well, do you want me to tell you about anything else I heard about Becky and John-Paul?" Delsey whispered.

Absolutely not! Megan's common sense wanted to shout. But her lips muttered, "You'd better."

* * * * *

Megan slowly walked into math class. She set her books on the desk and let her gaze wander to the front of the room where Becky Thorndyke sat. Becky was surrounded by three boys, but when she saw Megan, she waved at her. Megan offered a half-hearted smile and slipped into her seat. She nearly groaned out loud when she saw Becky swishing down the aisle toward her.

"Hi, Megan," Becky said. "I saw Audrey in Rinehauer's Department Store at the mall last weekend with her fiancé. They were picking out china patterns and looked so romantic."

Megan smiled but felt her insides churning. She kept imagining Becky's lips plastered against John-Paul's. "Yes, the wedding's not until June, but my sister's been shopping for china patterns since she was six."

Becky giggled. The sound irritated Megan like fingernails across a blackboard. Becky added, "Well, I can't imagine how you're keeping your mind on school what with being a bridesmaid and all."

Does everybody in the whole school know about my private life? Megan wondered. "The wedding's a long way off, Becky. There are a million other things to think about right now."

"Yes, but it's going to be such a big, fancy wedding. Is Brent going to wear his military uniform? And what about his groomsmen? Will they all be in uniform? I bet they'll look so romantic. Has Audrey picked out her dress yet? What does it look like?"

"Yes. Only the guys who attend the Citadel. And no." Megan answered Becky's questions in order, giving as little information as possible.

Audrey's wedding was none of Becky's business. But Megan knew that things were going to be like this until the wedding. After all, Audrey had been the most popular girl in junior high and high school. Everybody remembered her. She was homecoming queen two years in a row, she won a local beauty contest, and she was elected to the Teen Fashion Board at Rinehauer's Department Store. During her second year at Charleston's Junior College, Audrey met Brent and they fell madly in love. And now that Cinderella was marrying Prince Charming, people wanted to know every detail. *Too bad I'm supposed to be the news service*, Megan thought sourly.

"Well, I'd love to hear all about it. So tell me *everything*. Of course, I've got things to do today after school. Maybe some other day you can fill me in," Becky added, flapping her dark brown eyelashes. As Megan watched Becky walk back to her seat, she felt even angrier. *Yeah, and I just wonder what you're doing after school, Becky*, Megan thought.

That afternoon Megan walked home from school alone. She used to walk with John-Paul every day, but she was still mad at him for teasing her before gym class. When she arrived at the corner of her street, Megan waited for the traffic light to change. She glanced up the long stretch of sidewalk leading to the city park and squinted to see two figures walking hand-in-hand.

The muggy September air closed in around her. In the distance, Megan thought she recognized John-Paul and Becky. Megan felt a strange fluttering sensation in her chest, and a bad taste rose to her mouth. *Becky and John-Paul. Together.* She looked away and quickly crossed the street.

By the time Megan got home, she'd decided that things couldn't get worse. But she was wrong. Her mother was in bed again with another sick headache.

Three

November sunlight streamed through the stained-glass window over the altar of the huge church. Megan sat with her family in a cushioned oak pew. She fidgeted with the lace collar on her blue dress, feeling silly to be so dressed up. But she'd worn the dress to make her mother happy. After another long night with an awful headache, Mrs. McCaffery had awakened feeling somewhat better. A big family dinner was planned for after church. Brent was coming, and Megan knew that her mother wanted everything to be perfect.

Beside her, Thad squirmed and tugged at his necktie. Brent sat next to Audrey, who was wearing a black-and-white silk dress. Brent looked neat in his Citadel dress uniform of gray with gold braid. Megan couldn't deny that Audrey and Brent looked wonderful together. That very morning, when Megan and her mother were setting the table for dinner after church, Megan's mother had said, "Brent and Audrey will make a perfect couple."

Megan had wrinkled her nose. "How can you think that? All she knows how to do is primp. She can't even boil water without a recipe."

Her mother had laughed. "Your sister's like a flower raised in a greenhouse. She needs to be pampered and fussed over in order to bloom."

Megan lined up an ornate silver fork next to a white linen napkin. "Goodness knows, she's had a lifetime of *that*," Megan said sarcastically. "Audrey will go from being taken care of by you and Dad to being taken care of by Brent. I don't want to be that way. I want to *do* something with my life."

Mrs. McCaffery reached over a bouquet of autumn flowers and patted Megan's hand. "Everybody has a special calling," she said. "So try to be more tolerant of someone else's dreams without giving up on your own. You've got a good head on your shoulders, Megan. You're smart and you're practical. And you don't see life the way Audrey does. But it can be fun to be a girl, and it can be wonderful to fall in love."

Remembering the conversation with her mother caused Megan to twist uncomfortably in the pew. How did her mother always seem to know what was going on inside her head? She had such a knack for reaching into Megan and poking at her innermost secrets without prying or making fun of her.

Megan turned slightly to scan the rows behind her. She caught sight of John-Paul and his family across the aisle, two rows back. Next to John-Paul sat Becky Thorndyke. Megan turned back to face the front of the church, hoping they hadn't seen her looking at them. She twisted the ruffle on the cuff of her dress. *I can live without boys*, Megan decided. *I can do just fine on my own.*

After the service, Megan tapped her toe impatiently as her parents visited with friends in the Fellowship Hall. She wanted get out of there before she had to face Becky and John-Paul.

"Why, hi, Megan," Becky said as she tapped her shoulder.

Megan flinched. She turned and saw Becky standing there with her arm locked through John-Paul's. Megan noticed that he looked as uncomfortable as she felt.

"Hi," John-Paul mumbled and played with his tie.

"Oh, I just think your sister and her fiancé look so marvelous," Becky gushed.

"Marvelous," Megan agreed impatiently. *Aren't my parents ever going to leave?*

"I told John-Paul that I just can't wait 'til their wedding. Didn't I, John-Paul?"

22

He gave a half-nod.

Megan searched the thinning clusters of people and spied Thad. "Whoops … there's my brother telling me it's time to go," Megan said, backing away with a fake smile. "I'll … uh … catch you two in school tomorrow. I've got to run." Megan made a bee-line for Thad and seized him by his elbow. "Let's go," she commanded.

"Hey! What's going on? I'm not ready to leave."

"Oh, yes you are, buddy." She refused to loosen her grip and pushed him along in spite of his loud protests. Outside in the brisk November air, she paused and let go of Thad's arm.

"What's the big idea?" he shouted.

"I needed some fresh air, and I wanted you to come with me."

Thad screwed up his freckled nose and shook his head. "First you treat me like I'm a bug, then you tell me you want me to be with you. You girls are weird!"

Megan knew he was right. She did treat him according to what she needed from him. Inwardly, she cringed. What happened to the fun days of chasing around and not caring who was with whom? Why did seeing John-Paul and Becky cause her stomach to twist into knots? Why did everything have to change in order for Megan McCaffery to grow up?

Four

"Would you like another piece of peach pie, Brent?" asked Mrs. McCaffery.

"No, thank you, ma'am. I'm filled to the brim," Brent said, pushing himself away from the table and patting his stomach.

Megan also felt full. She wished she hadn't eaten so much, but everything tasted so good. There was something special about Sunday meals—the clink of china, the rich aroma of ham or beef, the sounds of conversation and laughter. Memories of Sunday dinner with her family around the beautifully set dining room table would follow her forever.

"It was perfect, honey," Megan's father told her mother.

Megan's mother smiled, but Megan noticed tiny lines forming at the corners of her mother's mouth. Megan knew her mother was coming down with another headache. "Let me clean up, Mom," she said, standing up to clear the table. "Thad, you can help."

Thad shot her a pouting, don't-boss-me-around look, but he helped anyway. Megan's mother sat back down. Megan listened to the low conversation as she carried plates and silverware through the swinging door.

"… and once you graduate from the Citadel in June, you'll make the Army your career?" Mr. McCaffery was asking Brent.

"Yes, sir. I've wanted to be an officer all my life. After the wedding and honeymoon, it's Army life for me and Audrey."

"Are you up to being an officer's wife, Audrey?"

"There's nothing I'd rather be than Brent's wife."

Megan almost dropped the salad bowl when she heard Audrey say those words. It sounded so corny. Megan rolled her eyes in disgust. Then she cornered Thad in the kitchen and made him load the dishwasher while she rinsed the plates and stacked them.

"This is girl's stuff," Thad grumbled.

"Work is work," Megan told him, running her mother's best china under a stream of warm water. "You do it until it gets done."

"Lincoln freed the slaves, you know."

"You're under ten, so you're not free," Megan teased and playfully splashed some water at him.

"Hey!" He darted back, ducked, and scooped up a handful of water from the running faucet and tossed it at her.

She squealed, laughed, and jumped backward. Then she grabbed a damp dishtowel and twisted it into a tight ribbon that cracked when she snapped it at his legs. "Now you're going to get it, Thad McCaffery."

"Watch out!" Thad yelled, picking up the long, wooden salad fork and holding it like a sword.

They pretended to fight in the middle of the kitchen floor. Thad jabbed with the fork and Megan tried to knock it out of his hand with the towel.

Just then, Megan's father walked in. "Hey, you two," he said good-naturedly. "Calm down. We've got company in the dining room."

Megan dropped the towel on the countertop. "Okay, Dad."

"Yeah, Dad. We're sorry," Thad said.

"What am I going to do with you, Megan? I've got one daughter who can't wait to grow up and one who wants to be a kid all her life," her father said with a smile. "Now, your mother's going upstairs to lie down for a while. And Audrey and Brent are going for a drive. I'll be in the den, so you two finish up this kitchen and do something quiet for a change."

"Yes, Dad," Megan and Thad said in unison.

He left and they quietly finished cleaning the kitchen. When the dishwasher was loaded and started, Thad escaped to watch TV. Megan changed into jeans and a sweater and went outside. She crossed the lawn, following a flagstone path to the white gazebo at the back of the yard. The sun shone through the latticework wood, casting checkerboard shadows over the concrete bench. With a sigh, Megan lowered herself onto the bench and gazed out over the vast expanse of lawn.

The garden blazed with the flowers of autumn. Yellow and white chrysanthemums and marigolds peeked from between the green shrubbery. Geraniums were clustered in bold bouquets of red and pink along the borders of the garden.

Megan pulled her knees to her chest and closed her arms around them.

"Are you alone?" John-Paul's voice broke into her thoughts. He walked into the gazebo and lowered himself onto the bench next to her.

"I *was* alone," she said.

"Then you won't mind if I join you."

"Make yourself comfortable," she said without much warmth in the invitation. She scooted to one side of the bench to give him room.

"You sure don't seem very friendly lately," he said, turning his head to the side and causing his soft, black hair to flop on his forehead.

"I figured you had a new friend in Becky."

"So what? Can't I have more than one friend?"

"Do you like her?" Megan blurted the question. Immediately she wished she could take it back, because it sounded as if she *cared* whether he liked Becky or not.

"She's all right." He picked up a twig that had fallen through the latticework. "So what if I do like her? Are you jealous?"

A knot formed in Megan's stomach. "No way! It's just that we're friends, and I'm curious. I mean, Becky has a way of hanging all over you that, well, that looks … sort of silly."

"It doesn't bother me to have her hanging around," he said nonchalantly.

"I was just trying to describe how it looks to everybody else."

"What do I care? The guys at school think Becky and I look good together."

"Well, that should bring Becky true peace of mind—knowing that all the guys approve. I sure wouldn't like to know what all the guys were saying about me," she sniffed.

The setting sun shone on John-Paul's face, turning his skin a coppery-gold color. "And what makes you think you aren't being talked about, Megan McCaffery?" John-Paul said with a mischievous smile.

Megan felt her face redden. "You talk about me? You and your stupid friends stand around and talk about me? How dare you!"

John-Paul laughed, "Boy, I sure can get a rise out of you, can't I, Megan Sue?"

She wanted to punch him and knock the smugness out of him. She balled her fist, but he jumped off the bench, laughing.

"I ought to sock you," she said through clenched teeth.

"Why?"

"Because," she said.

"I was only teasing you. I used to be able to tease you, and all you'd do was tease me back. Now it bothers you. Why?"

Megan felt confused by his question. She didn't really know why.

The sound of her father's voice urgently calling her name startled her. "Here, Dad!" She bolted off the bench, her heart thudding as she hurried into the yard to meet him.

Mr. McCaffery came running across the lawn, his hair mussed, his eyes full of alarm. "Megan! Come quick! We've got to hurry. I've just found your mother unconscious on the floor. I've called an ambulance and it's on its way right now!"

Five

Megan twisted her hands in her lap. She shifted from side to side in the gray upholstered chair where she sat in the conference room of the Charleston hospital. Had it only been forty-eight hours since the ambulance had rushed her mother to the emergency room? Had it been only two days since she'd been admitted and endless tests had been performed on her? For Megan, it seemed like weeks.

Her eyes darted from her father's worried face to Audrey's pale expression to Thad's wide-eyed stare. Dr. Van Avery sat opposite them. He was one of the best neurologists in the South, so the family was grateful that he was the doctor in charge of Mrs. McCaffery's case. He was a small man with light brown hair and a moustache. His kind, brown eyes peered at them from behind wire-rimmed glasses.

"I'm glad you all are here, Mr. McCaffery," Dr. Van Avery said.

"We're a family, Doctor," Mr. McCaffery said strongly. "My wife and I would like you to explain to our children exactly what's going on. We don't believe in keeping secrets from our children. Please, tell them what you've told us."

The doctor swiveled his chair to face Megan, Audrey, and Thad. He cleared his throat and began. "I know you must have many questions about what's been happening to your mother since she was admitted two days ago."

"It's the headaches, right? She's been having them for months," Megan said.

"They're awful," Audrey added. "She'd have to go to bed because they hurt so much."

"I'd read to her and get her wet washcloths," Megan added shyly. "Sometimes that helped. We knew they were bad, but they're really bad, aren't they?"

Dr. Van Avery studied Megan carefully before saying, "Many things can cause headaches. Stress, hormonal changes, high blood pressure … ," he listed, using his fingers to count them off. "But your mother seems to have none of these problems. So, we have had to look for something else."

"But she said that headaches run in her family, so maybe you're looking for nothing. I mean, maybe they'll go away on their own." Megan's hopeful comment caused Thad to nod vigorously.

Dr. Van Avery shook his head slowly. "Perfectly normal people don't have a seizure and collapse and have to be rushed to the hospital."

"Is that what happened?" Thad blurted. "Dad just found her lying on the floor."

"That's what our tests have shown. Yesterday we performed an electroencephalogram—that's a test that draws a picture of a person's brainwave patterns. And your mother's weren't normal. We also did a CAT scan."

"You let a cat look at my mother?" Thad's questions made everyone giggle, which relieved some of the tension.

Megan didn't know exactly what a CAT scan was, but she knew it didn't have anything to do with a real cat.

"A CAT scanner is a giant machine that lets us see inside a person with X-rays. It shows us a three-dimensional picture of the area in question. Then we can study the picture and look for abnormalities."

"Did it hurt her?" asked Thad.

"Not at all. She just lies very still on a table that moves her through a tunnel. The X-rays are taken as she goes through."

"Oh." Thad nodded as if giving his permission. "I guess that was all right to do."

Megan was glad Thad had asked. She'd wanted to know, too, but she didn't want the doctor to think she was stupid.

"Tell them what your tests have shown, Doctor," Mr. McCaffery said. His fingers were laced together and were white at the knuckles.

The doctor flipped through the manila folder again, shuffled the papers, and finally said, "We suspect that your mother has a brain tumor."

Megan's face drained of color at the doctor's words, and she felt sick to her stomach.

"Your tests say that my mother has a tumor growing in her head?" Audrey asked, blinking back tears. "What are you going to do about it?"

"My colleague, Dr. Nash, is an excellent neurosurgeon who'll operate—"

Thad leaped to his feet. "You're going to cut open my mother's head? No! Don't do that!"

Megan reached over and took Thad's wrist. She pulled him back into his chair. "Let him explain, Thad."

Thad scooted back against the seat cushion.

"We have to, Thad," Dr. Van Avery said kindly. "We have to look at the tumor. But did you know that your brain has no nerve endings, so you can't feel anything inside the brain itself?"

Thad shook his head in disbelief, and Megan found the information unbelievable, too.

"There are nerve endings in the scalp," explained the doctor. "That's why it hurts to get your hair pulled."

Thad shot Megan a knowing glance, and she blushed, remembering the times she'd grabbed a handful of his hair during one of their fights.

Dr. Van Avery continued, "But the brain itself can't feel a thing. Sometimes, after we give a local anesthetic, we operate on a person's brain while he or she is wide awake."

"Will my mom be awake when you operate on her?" Thad asked, wide-eyed.

"No, your mother will be asleep when we operate. We may have to remove the tumor once a biopsy is performed."

"A biopsy?" asked Megan.

"I'll take out a few cells from the tumor and send them to the lab. The people there will look at the cells to find out if the tumor is cancerous."

For a moment no one spoke. The silence in the room was smothering. Megan felt as if all the air had been pushed out of her lungs. *Cancer.* She understood what that word meant. She'd read in her biology book about rats that had cancer. And once a teacher at her elementary school had to quit because she had cancer. The teacher died a few months later.

"And if it is cancerous, … what then, Dr. Van Avery?" Mr. McCaffery's voice was very soft.

"First, we remove it. Then we fight with everything available. Radiation treatment begins. Maybe chemotherapy. It'll depend."

Megan's stomach felt queasy. "How long will my mother be in the hospital?"

"She'll recover quickly from the basic surgery and go home. But if the tumor is cancerous, she must come in on an outpatient basis for her therapy. She'll resume as normal a life as possible and be as active as she feels she can be. She'll have to watch her exposure to the sun, and she may be tired a lot, but she'll be at home with all of you."

"Can't you just take out the tumor after the biopsy?" Megan asked. If this Dr. Nash was so good, then why couldn't he cut out the whole tumor as long as he was operating?

"Do you know how tiny a cell is? We can't even see them with the naked eye. We have to use microscopes to look at them. Because they are so small, we can't be certain that we've gotten every single cell when we do an operation. If the tumor is cancerous, what we doctors call *malignant*, then we must be positive that we get rid of all of it, or it will grow back. Or it may move to another part of her body. That's why radiation treatment will be so important. Cancerous cells don't like radiation, but normal cells can survive it."

Again, the room went silent. Megan heard the blood rushing in her ears and felt her palms growing clammy. "When are you going to do all of this?"

"We'll keep her on medications for a few days to prevent any more seizures. Then we'll do the surgery, maybe toward the first of next week. Dr. Nash and I are studying your mother's reports."

"Can I see my mom?" Thad asked, chewing on his lower lip. Megan knew he was on the verge of tears.

"Absolutely. I'll give special instructions for you to get into her room, Thad, even though the hospital says visitors have to be over twelve. All of you can visit her this evening."

Sensing that the meeting was over, Megan stood up. Her legs felt weak and rubbery. She sucked in a deep breath. She still had a question, but she couldn't voice it yet. She couldn't ask the one question that haunted her most of all. She filed out of the conference room with her family and rode down the elevator. All the way home in the car, the question nagged at her. What if the surgery and the radiation didn't work? What would happen to her mother then?

* * * * *

"Gee, Megan, I'm so sorry about your mother." John-Paul's words sounded kind. Around them, the sounds in the school cafeteria roared.

Megan poked the peas on her plate and squished them with the back of her fork. "Yeah. It's hard for me to think about some ugly thing growing inside my mother's head. How did it start growing? And why?"

John-Paul couldn't really answer her questions, so instead he asked, "Are you okay?"

Megan shoved her tray aside and rested her chin on a balled-up fist on top of the table. "I don't know. It's too much to think about."

"Does anybody else know?"

"Not yet." Megan looked at John-Paul. "You won't tell anyone, will you? I ... I just don't want everybody talking about it all over the school. Not yet. Not until we know … if it's …" She couldn't get the word out.

"I won't tell," he promised. "Do you want me to walk home with you after school?"

Megan was glad he asked. They'd fallen out of the habit of walking together ever since Becky Thorndyke had entered his life. In spite of how much they'd fought lately, she had to admit that she missed him. "That would be all right."

"Then I'll meet you at the corner next to the gym." He stood up, stacked his tray on hers, and picked up both of them.

"I can carry my own tray," she said.

"I've got it. But if you want to make things even, I'll let you carry my books home." His smile lit up his face.

She smiled back. "See you after school."

Later, they walked home under overcast skies. A cold breeze ruffled Megan's silky-fine hair. John-Paul was quiet during the walk. He seemed to understand Megan's need to keep to herself.

They turned into the driveway of her home and sauntered up to the porch. Megan turned and faced John-Paul for a moment, searching for words to thank him. Then the door jerked open and Audrey emerged, her face pale and her eyes red-rimmed.

"Oh, Megan," she said. "Thank heaven you're home. Dad called from the hospital. They decided not to wait to do Mom's surgery. Dr. Nash is going to operate the day after tomorrow."

Six

"Do you think you can read all those in just two days?" John-Paul skeptically eyed the stack of books on Megan's dining room table.

Megan paused from her reading and peered at him over the pile of medical texts. "I can if people stop jabbering at me. Did you stop by for some particular reason?" Megan felt bad that she couldn't control her anger. Just yesterday, she had felt so warm toward him. But now she just wanted to be alone so she could read all she could about cancer and her mother's condition.

"I thought you'd like to know that my mom and sister are going to wait with you tomorrow at the hospital during your mother's operation. I asked if I could stay, too, but Mom said no, that I had to go to school."

Megan was both touched and sorry. She was touched because he'd thought enough of her family to want to be with them throughout the long wait of the surgery—and sorry because of her angry words.

It would have been nice to have him near, especially if the news was bad. "Well, that's nice of you, but we'll manage."

He let his eyes wander to her open book. "Are all these about medicine?"

"Every one."

"Where'd you get them?"

"From the public library. Audrey took me after we got the news about them moving up Mom's surgery."

"Are you going to take over your mother's case?"

Megan smirked at him. "It never hurts to find out all you can about a topic."

"What are you finding out?"

"I'm reading about tumors. You know, a lot of them are benign. That means not cancerous. If it's benign, then they just snip it out and that's the end of it."

"And if it isn't?"

She looked hard at the book in front of her. "Then I'll read about the newest treatments. I want to make sure my mother has the best."

"She's got doctors to decide that."

Megan closed her book with a bang. "Come on, John-Paul. I've got a lot of reading to do between now and tomorrow's surgery. I haven't got time to chat all day."

He ignored her and sat down in the chair across from her. "I'll read along with you."

"That's not necessary."

He flashed a smile. "No problem, Megan Sue. I don't mind at all. Besides, it's cold outside and there's only algebra waiting for me at home."

"Suit yourself," she replied, and then returned to reading the open book.

John-Paul studied the titles on the bindings of several texts before choosing one. They read together quietly, the faint drone of the furnace humming in the background. It was John-Paul who broke Megan's concentration several minutes later. "This isn't very pleasant reading."

"Why? What'd you read?"

He closed the book and rocked back on the chair legs. "It's just depressing to read about disease and stuff, that's all."

Her eyes narrowed. "What'd you read?"

"A bunch of stuff about untreated malignant brain tumors."

"What about them?"

"Sometimes the patient goes blind and deaf, and then goes into a coma and dies. And it doesn't necessarily hurt, either. One minute you can see. The next minute, you're blind." He pondered the thought. "I'd hate to be blind."

Megan shuddered. "Well, that won't happen to Mom, because they're treating her. And besides, I'm betting it's benign."

"Me, too," John-Paul said enthusiastically. "Tell you what. I'll buy you a hamburger and a milkshake after you get home from the hospital tomorrow to celebrate. That's how sure I am that everything's going to be just fine."

"You're buying?" Megan's eyes met his. "Well, then you'd better bring along a fortune, John-Paul Harrison, because I plan to eat everything in sight. Double cheeseburger, double fries, and a king-size milkshake."

"You always did have the appetite of a horse."

She remembered the time they joined the pie-eating contest to raise funds for a project in the fourth grade. Megan won the contest. But she never told John-Paul that she was sick that night. "So bring your bank, Harrison. I *still* eat like a horse."

Hours later, while she was changing her clothes to go visit her mother at the hospital, Megan realized that John-Paul had kind of asked her for a date. *But not a real date,* she told herself. *He's just trying to help me take my mind off Mom's operation.*

But all the same, Megan wondered what Becky Thorndyke might think.

* * * * *

Megan slipped into the dim quiet of her mother's hospital room. The room smelled like medicine. A hose attached to a mask hung on the wall next to her mother's bed.

"Hi, Mom," Megan whispered, standing beside the bed.

"Hi, baby." Mrs. McCaffery reached out and Megan took her hand. Her fingers were cold. "I've seen the others. I was wondering when you'd come."

"I—I wanted to be last," Megan said. "No particular reason." As her eyes adjusted to the dimness, Megan noticed how sterile the room looked. "So, are you ready for tomorrow?" she asked, still holding her mother's hand.

Mrs. McCaffery's other hand touched the soft, cotton-knit hat hugging her head. "I hope so. They shaved my head, Megan."

45

Megan was shocked for a moment. *Shaved her head! Of course—for the surgery.* She remembered her mom's soft auburn curls. "It's going to be all right, Mom. I just know it is."

"I told your father that you didn't have to wait here at the hospital for the results of the operation. It will be a long, boring day."

"Mom, there's no place for us to be except together. Besides, I promised Thad a game of cards while we wait. And someone's got to keep an eye on Audrey. You know how she goes to pieces in a crisis."

"You are a rock, aren't you, Megan?"

Megan shrugged. "Rock-headed," she said. "At least that's what Audrey always says."

"After the surgery, I'll be in the recovery room. So I don't know when I'll see you again."

"Whenever they let me, I'll be here."

Mr. McCaffery poked his head into the door-way. "It's my turn to say good night, Megan."

She squeezed her mother's hand. "Good night, Mom. I wished on a star for you tonight."

Her mother's smile was soft. "Then I know everything will come out fine."

Megan's vision went blurry with a film of tears. She hurried out of the room, and then leaned against the corridor wall until she could control her crying. Tomorrow was just around the corner. Megan didn't know if she could hold out that long.

* * * * *

The wait was nerve-racking. The private waiting room felt uncomfortable, even though it was cheerfully painted and had vending machines, a TV, a game table, sofas, and chairs. Megan played a half-hearted game of cards with Thad and Brent. Audrey and John-Paul's sister, Rosemary, huddled together looking at bridal magazines. Mr. McCaffery paced like a caged lion. Mrs. Harrison sat doing needle-point and offering to get coffee for Mr. McCaffery every so often.

The first thing that morning, a tall, thin Dr. Nash had greeted them, along with Dr. Van Avery. Dr. Nash assured them that he'd be back with a full report as soon as the surgery was finished. That had been hours ago, and the later it got, the more tense the atmosphere became in the waiting room.

"Is it absolutely necessary for you to sit there and crack your knuckles?" Megan snapped at Thad over the board game.

"Well, I can't decide where to move."

She smirked. "Well, hurry up, Thaddeus."

"Don't call me that," he demanded. "Why did Mom have to have some relative named Thaddeus anyway?"

"He was a colonel in the Civil War and you should be proud of the name."

"Like you're proud of Megan Sue?" Thad needled.

"Cut it out!" Their father's sharp command silenced them both immediately.

"Well, I'm bored stiff with this stupid old game anyway," Megan said. She walked over to the TV. She clicked it on with the remote, watched a few minutes of a game show, and clicked it off. The game was so easy that even she could answer all of the questions. Why did people watch it anyway?

The door to the waiting room swung open and every eye watched Dr. Nash as he entered the room. He was still dressed in his green surgical clothes, his hair covered by a surgical cap, and his mask dangling from his neck.

"Your wife's doing well," he said, directing his comments to Mr. McCaffery. "She's in recovery, and you can see her when she's moved to intensive care. I'll let you know."

"And the tumor?"

Megan's heart was hammering so hard against the sides of her ribcage that she thought it might break through.

Dr. Nash said, "We sent tissue samples to the lab and got the biopsy report back. I'm sorry to say that the tumor is malignant. I removed all of it that I could without damaging the surrounding brain tissue, but she'll have to begin radiation therapy immediately."

Seven

Mrs. McCaffery recovered from surgery over the Thanksgiving holiday. It was the loneliest holiday Megan had ever spent. Mr. McCaffery spent the day at the hospital with his wife. Audrey went off to Columbus to be with Brent and his family. Thad ate at Billy's, and Megan stayed with John-Paul and his mother and sister.

Following the recuperation, Mrs. McCaffery became an outpatient and began her radiation treatments. Two times a week, she went to the hospital where technicians bombarded her head with massive doses of radiation in an effort to destroy the malignant cancer cells. It seemed to Megan that the therapy was as much her mother's enemy as the cancer. It sapped her mom's energy and made her nauseous. She was so exhausted that she slept most of the time.

"We'll treat her for four weeks," Dr. Van Avery told the family. "Then I'll do tests to see how much the remaining tumor has shrunk. After that, she'll resume as normal a life as possible. She'll feel better, too," the doctor assured the family. "She is very determined and has a positive attitude. I think she'll be up and around by Christmas Day. Let's look to that as our goal."

As the Christmas season approached, Megan realized how difficult it was not having her mother participate in the usual breakneck pace of the holiday season. Mr. McCaffery and Audrey did most of the Christmas shopping. Megan and Thad decorated the house. Audrey and Megan assumed most of the household chores, including planning the Christmas dinner.

Megan and Audrey were scurrying around the kitchen, preparing the holiday dinner that would celebrate the McCaffery's being together again as a family. Megan felt happy, even though Audrey was barking orders at her every few minutes.

"Megan, can't you peel those potatoes faster? At the rate you're moving, the turkey will be done and stone-cold before the potatoes ever get boiled and mashed."

"Hold your horses. I've only got two hands, you know. Stop nagging me!"

"How are you coming with the green beans, Mom? Is it too much work?" Audrey's voice turned kind as she addressed their mother, who was seated at the counter snapping green beans into a bowl.

"I'm doing just fine, girls. We'll have dinner on the table by four this afternoon for sure. Don't worry." Her mother was terribly thin. She wore a bright red, woolen hat to cover her baldness. Her hair had not begun to grow back after the operation. The radiation therapy had prevented it. But Mrs. McCaffery prepared the beans happily, humming a cheerful Christmas carol under her breath.

Mr. McCaffery ambled into the kitchen to get some coffee and looked at the messy room. "Did you girls have a war in here?" he said jokingly.

"Dad, please, it's not easy getting a whole Christmas dinner together. Is Brent doing all right?" Audrey asked.

"Brent's throwing the football outside with Thad and John-Paul. They've already ridden the new bikes around the neighborhood five times."

Megan half-wished she could be outside tossing the football. Cooking was no fun. Especially with Audrey giving the orders. She diced the potatoes and deposited them in a big pot of water. She turned the burner on "high" and asked to be excused for a minute.

"Now don't you go running off, Megan McCaffery," Audrey warned sternly. "Is the table set?"

"It's set," Megan assured her sister before escaping through the swinging door. Wearily, she slipped into the living room where the Christmas tree stood. A Christmas angel topped the tree. Megan inhaled the tangy sent of the pine needles and flopped on the couch. Then she looked at the layers of presents and yards of discarded paper and ribbon. She'd been up since six in the morning. Now that the initial excitement was over, Megan felt her energy begin to drain.

She had gotten lots of presents. She loved what her parents had given her—a cashmere sweater and wool dress slacks. But the best gift of all was having her mother home. Megan dropped to her knees and crawled toward the tree, studying the bright collection of hats and scarves they'd bought to cover her mom's head for the rest of her treatments, until her hair would grow back.

Megan glanced around the room and made sure she was alone. Then she reached far behind the tree for the only unopened gift, the one she'd hidden beneath the red skirt concealing the tree stand. Her fingers closed around a small, foil-wrapped box.

This was the present Megan had bought for John-Paul. She turned it over in her hands, wondering if she had lost her nerve to give it to him. What would he say? Had he gotten something for her?

They'd often given each other Christmas gifts, but those had been "kid" things, toys or books. This was a *real* gift, one she'd bought especially for him. Inside the box was a sterling silver keychain with his initials—*JPH*—engraved on it. Next month, he'd turn fifteen and get his learner's permit. Now he would have his very own keychain. What would he say when he opened it?

A dark thought crossed her mind. Had he gotten something for Becky Thorndyke? Megan made a face, thinking of how Becky would make such a big deal of it at school. "I hope you had better sense, John-Paul Harrison," Megan muttered under her breath.

"Megan!" Audrey's voice sliced through Megan's thoughts. "I need help. Where are you?"

Megan sprang to her feet, shoved the box deep into the pocket of her jeans, and sprinted out of the room. "Don't have a fit! Can't a person take a break?"

Audrey stood in front of Megan with her hands on her hips. "Mom's gone up to rest, and the potatoes have boiled all over the stove because you turned the burner too high. And everything's going wrong. The stuffing keeps dripping out of the turkey, and the yeast rolls won't rise, and the candied yams are all gooey and—" Audrey paused to sniff the air. Something was burning! "Oh, no!" Audrey cried, running into the kitchen with Megan fast on her heels.

Smoke leaked from the oven door. Audrey shrieked, "My turkey! Oh, my beautiful turkey!"

Megan watched as Audrey flung open the door. Dark, heavy smoke poured out. Running feet pounded into the kitchen. "What happened?" Mr. McCaffery, John-Paul, and Thad asked in unison.

"It's–it's burned ..." Audrey wailed, jamming two oven mitts on and lifting out the charred remains of the turkey.

"How'd that happen?" Megan demanded.

"I–I don't know ... I put it in just like it said on the side of the box of aluminum foil ..." Audrey managed between sobs after she'd set the pan down.

Brent put his arms around her shoulders and drew her close to his chest.

Megan picked up the box and read, "Cook at four hundred and fifty degrees *if* the turkey is wrapped in foil. It wasn't wrapped in foil, Audrey. No wonder it burned."

Audrey cried even harder.

Mr. McCaffery ran his fingers through his hair. "Calm down, honey. It's not the end of the world, you know."

Megan exchanged glances with Thad and John-Paul. She mumbled, "It's just the end of Christmas dinner."

Her father turned toward her. "Well, everything else looks good. Megan, look in the refrigerator and see if there's any meat in there we can substitute."

Megan walked to the refrigerator and sorted through a collection of salads and pies. She pulled out a package that she tossed with a thud on the counter. "Two pounds of hotdogs," she said cheerfully. "And don't worry, Audrey. At least they're *turkey* hotdogs."

* * * * *

In the long run, the dinner wasn't quite the disaster it started out to be. They roasted the hotdogs in the fireplace. Even their mother came downstairs and nibbled on a hotdog while curled up in the corner of the sofa, an afghan stretched over her lap.

As twilight was falling, Megan bundled up in

her coat and gloves and walked down to the gazebo with John-Paul. She breathed in the frosty air and looked up at the stars.

"I wish it would have snowed," she said. "Someday I'm going to have a white Christmas, just like the one in the song."

"You'd have to leave Charleston," John-Paul observed. "We only get flurries. It's been three years since we had any snow stay on the ground." His shoulders brushed against hers. In the cold air, his presence warmed her, making her insides feel fluttery. "Uh—Megan … ," he began. "Megan—uh—I haven't had a chance to see you all day …"

She turned to face him. Megan couldn't see his eyes in the darkness. "Yeah. It's been a hectic day," she said.

"I didn't want you to think I'd forgotten it was Christmas and all."

Her heart began to hammer. The box in her pocket was probably mangled and misshapen by now. "I know it's Christmas," she said.

"I got you a present."

"You did?" Megan asked.

"Well, of course." He reached into his pocket and pulled out a box about the same size as the one she had for him. "I—uh—hope you like it," he said.

Her hands were trembling as she took it. "Thank you."

"Open it."

She peeled off the paper and opened the box. Starlight glinted off a round golden charm. "It's a softball," she whispered.

He cleared his throat. "It's for the chain you wear around your neck. That is, if you want to put it on the chain," he added quickly.

"Of course, I do! Oh, John-Paul, thank you so much."

He jammed his hands down into his coat pockets. "I—uh—just saw it and thought you'd like it."

"I love it." She did, too. Not just because it was so pretty, but even more because he had given it to her. She fished out her gift for him. "I'm sorry this is all mashed," she said as she tried to straighten the once-beautiful box. "But here. This is for you."

Megan watched as he unwrapped and removed the keychain.

"All right!" John-Paul said, holding the keychain up in the moonlight. "This is terrific. Thanks a million, Megan."

They stood admiring their gifts. The silence was awkward for Megan. She didn't know what else to say.

She stepped backward. "I–I need to go back inside … ," she said through chattering teeth. "Audrey and Brent were supposed to make some kind of family announcement …" Megan drew away and jogged toward the house. "Thanks for the present, John-Paul. I'll see you tomorrow." She ran quickly into the house, kicking herself the whole time for taking his gift and then running away.

"Megan, where have you been?" Audrey asked the moment she came into the dining room. Her family was eating pie around the table.

"I–I was just getting some fresh air—"

"Brent and I have some news," Audrey interrupted, ignoring Megan's flushed cheeks and confusing explanation. "We were just telling Mom and Dad our special news." Her eyes fastened on Brent's smiling face. "We've decided not to wait until June to get married. We're moving the wedding up to the end of March."

Eight

"That's wonderful," Mrs. McCaffery said warmly.

"Yes … yes," Mr. McCaffery concurred. "Of course, if you think you can get it together by then."

"March? That's only three months from now," Thad ticked off on his fingers.

"But why?" Megan's demanding question stopped the chatter in the room.

"Why what?" Audrey asked.

"Why do you want to move it up? What's wrong with June?"

"Why not?" Audrey countered. "We think it's silly to wait when we could be married much sooner."

Megan sent her sister an angry look. "Well, I'm against it." She turned on her heel and headed up the stairs, leaving her family stunned.

At the top of the stairs, she went straight to her room. Megan slammed the door and stretched across her bed. She didn't even turn on the light.

How dare Audrey move up her wedding! she thought. *Doesn't she think about anybody but herself? Doesn't she realize how much work she is shoving onto Mom in half the time?*

A knock sounded at the door. "Megan, it's me, Mom. Please let me in."

She scooted off the bed, turned on the light, and opened the door. "Hi, Mom," she said without much enthusiasm.

"What was that all about?"

"What?"

"Don't play games, Megan." Mrs. McCaffery lowered herself onto Megan's bed.

A pang shot through Megan. "Your red hat doesn't match that bathrobe, Mom. We got you lots of hats for Christmas. Couldn't you find one that matched?" Megan began pacing the floor.

"So that's what's bothering you, is it? My hat doesn't match." Mrs. McCaffery patted the bed next to her. "Come sit down before you wear a hole in the carpet."

Megan sat down, but set her jaw in defiance.

"You know, Megan McCaffery, you remind me so much of your great-grandmother Taylor on my side."

"You mean the one who burned the farm?"

61

Mrs. McCaffery nodded. "You remember the story. Her husband had been killed in the War Between the States, and the Yankees were setting up an offensive line north of Charleston. When she heard they were planning to use her farm for a command post, she burned it to the ground, even though four generations of Taylors had lived there and it was all she owned in this world. Then she packed up her kids and walked all the way across the county to relocate in Charleston. After the war, the carpetbaggers bought the farm for back taxes."

"So what? It was her choice."

"Well, maybe if she'd been a little less hardheaded, a little more tolerant and diplomatic, we'd still have the farm in the family today. But she couldn't tolerate what she couldn't control. So she abandoned everything and lost it all."

Megan screwed up her face in confusion. "How's that like me?"

Megan's mother picked at a tuft on Megan's bedspread. "I've got cancer, Megan. I can't make it go away by wishing it were gone. I don't know if the radiation treatments will work. I do know that I want to see Audrey get married—and that by moving the wedding up, I'll have a better chance of doing that."

Megan squirmed. Her mother had hit on just what was bothering Megan. By moving up the wedding date, Audrey was suggesting that all of their hopes for a complete cure were for nothing. "It's too much work to get accomplished in three months," Megan grumbled.

"Not if we all pitch in."

Megan sprang off the bed. "Well, count me out! I don't care about Audrey's stupid wedding! She and Brent can elope. That'd be best for all of us anyway. Let her and Rosemary plan the wedding. Let them do everything. I don't even want to be in the stupid thing!"

"Megan, you really don't mean that."

"Yes, I really do, Mom." Megan nodded vigorously. "I mean every word of it. Just tell her to find herself another bridesmaid, because I won't be one!"

* * * * *

When January came, Megan was eager to get back in school. With plans for Audrey's wedding going full-tilt, the house always seemed to be in an uproar. School was the only place where Megan could escape the constant talk about invitations and dresses and flowers and honeymoons. Audrey had generally ignored Megan's decision not to be in the wedding.

Just the other day, she had said to Megan, "Since it's a spring ceremony, Rosemary and I were thinking about bridesmaids' dresses in shades of pink and lilac. What do you think about that, Megan? With your coloring, you'd look great in lilac. Don't you think so?"

"I told you, Audrey. I don't want to be in your wedding. Please pick another bridesmaid to fill in for me."

"Let's see, Rosemary will be my maid of honor, and I've asked Brent's older sister and my friend from the office and you. That's four. Each of you will wear a shade of rose, pink, lilac, and lavender. That'll be really pretty, won't it?"

Megan's patience wore thin. "Audrey, pick someone else to be in my color, because I won't be in it."

"Don't be silly. You'll change your mind." Then Audrey had walked confidently out of the room, while Megan stewed over her sister's stubbornness.

Megan continued to read everything she could find about cancer. John-Paul found her in the library after school one day, her nose buried in a magazine. He asked, "What are you doing? Have they called you in to consult on your mother's case?"

Ever since Christmas, she had kept a distance

from John-Paul. In some ways, that night in the gazebo was like a dream. She kept trying to forget the strange feelings she'd had about him. "Very funny, John-Paul. I told you a long time ago that I want to find out all I can about cancer. Those doctors have lots of patients and my mother isn't their only concern."

He sprawled out in the chair next to hers at the library table. His black pullover sweater made his eyes look even darker. For a few seconds she tried to ignore him, self-consciously fingering the softball charm attached to her necklace. "Is there something you want, John-Paul?" she finally asked.

He wrinkled his forehead, as if measuring words before he spoke them. "How's your mother doing?"

Megan shrugged. She found it difficult to share her fears about her mother, even with John-Paul. "She has good days and bad ones. Sometimes the radiation makes her sick. She sleeps a lot and gets confused. She can't even remember the day of the week. It's sort of like living with stranger. She looks like Mom, but sometimes—" Her words caught in her throat. "The treatments end in a few weeks, then they'll do another CAT scan. If the radiation did its thing, the tumor might be gone."

"Seems simple enough," John-Paul said.

"It isn't. If it starts growing back, there's not much more they can do. I read that you can only give a person so much radiation or it becomes dangerous. It can cause cancer, too."

John-Paul let out a low whistle. "Seems like you can't win."

"That's why I have to keep reading," Megan said, shuffling the magazine. "I want to know *all* the possibilities." She was aware of his eyes on her. "Is there anything else?" Her tone was sharper than she meant it to be. Actually, it felt good to have him near her, even though it was harder to concentrate.

"Rosemary said Audrey wants me to be a groomsman for her wedding."

Megan slapped the magazine against the table. "Brent has lots of friends at the Citadel to be groomsmen. Why is Audrey pestering you?"

A grin spread across his face. "My talent and charm, I guess. Don't you want me to be in the wedding?"

She sniffed. "It makes no difference to me. But I'm not going to be part of it, so don't try and talk me into it."

"Never. I'll wave at you from the altar when I'm standing up front with whomever they pick as your replacement."

She thought about him walking up the aisle with a girl dressed in lilac holding onto his arm. Who would Audrey choose in her place? The imaginary girl faded as Becky Thorndyke walked up the library table and said, "Hi, Megan. Hi, John-Paul." Becky flapped her dark eyelashes toward John-Paul and touched his shoulder as if she owned it. "Thanks for waiting for me."

He cleared his throat. "No problem."

Megan pretended she didn't care. Becky looked at her and said, "I've never told you how sorry I am about your mother, Megan. But I'm really sorry. All the cheerleaders are sorry, and if there's anything we can do …"

It irked Megan that she was the topic of conversation of Becky and her crowd. What did Becky expect? Was she supposed to ask them to say a get-well cheer? "She's doing much better," Megan said.

"Well, if there's anything I can do … ," Becky said. When Megan had nothing more to say, Becky turned her attention to John-Paul. "I'm ready to walk home now, so if you'll excuse us—" She gave Megan a too-sweet smile.

John-Paul rose to his feet, scraping the legs of the chair on the bare floor. Something gnawed at Megan's stomach. It made her want to shove Becky flat on the floor. It was an ugly feeling and Megan hated it, but she didn't know what to do about it. She uttered short good-byes and watched them leave the library. Megan felt alone and unwanted.

Suddenly, she understood why her great-grandmother could have willingly burned her farm to the ground. It was better than having it overrun by unwelcome strangers—a whole lot better.

Nine

The newest crop of X-rays showed that the tumor had shrunk. The McCaffery family was ecstatic! They celebrated by ordering pizza and putting candles on it like a birthday cake. By February, Mrs. McCaffery seemed like her old self, even though her energy level was still low. Megan didn't care, just as long as her mother was getting well.

Plans for the wedding were in full swing. The dining room table was heaped with invitations, envelopes, stamps, and address lists from the McCaffery's and Brent's families. Megan avoided direct discussions about the event and quickly left the room whenever Audrey started talking about it.

Thad asked her one night when they were alone watching television, "Why don't you want to be in Audrey's wedding? It doesn't seem right, you not being in it and all."

She didn't know how to explain it to him. She wasn't even sure *she* knew why except that it was one small area she seemed to have control over. "I just don't want to," Megan finally told him.

Thad accepted her remark with a shrug, and he watched the show for a long while before he broke into her concentration again. "If Mom gets sick again and Audrey's married, do you ever think about who'll take care of us?"

Megan turned her eyes from the screen to Thad's face. He looked so small and vulnerable, his expression full of worry. "Mom's not going to get sick again," Megan said gently.

"But just in case."

"Dad'll be here."

"Dad works. Can you cook?"

"Is that what's been worrying you, Thad McCaffery? Are you afraid you'll starve to death?" She tried to make it sound funny. "I can make grilled cheese and heat a can of soup, you know."

He wrinkled his nose. "Is that all?"

"Well, I can always get some recipes from Audrey."

Thad fell dramatically off the couch onto the floor and clutched his stomach. "You mean, the queen of food poisoning?"

Megan burst out laughing and fell to the floor next to him, moaning in agony as if she'd been poisoned. "Yeah, Audrey's idea of home cooking is burning the house down."

"What's the best thing Audrey makes for dinner?" Thad asked, rolling on the floor giggling.

"Reservations at a restaurant," Megan answered.

Megan's sides ached from laughing. The two of them rolled around in a helpless tangle, until Audrey walked in and demanded, "What's so funny?"

Megan and Thad exchanged glances, and then burst into fresh waves of hysterical giggles. "Funny TV show," Megan gasped.

Audrey peered at the screen and finally shrugged. "What's so funny about an aspirin commercial?"

Thad and Megan dissolved again. "You would have to have been here from the beginning," she said, wiping tears from her cheeks.

"Yeah," Thad agreed. "It wouldn't be funny at all if we tried to explain it."

Audrey flipped her hair off her shoulders and left the room. Megan and Thad returned to watching TV, but every time they so much as glanced at each other, they began to giggle.

*　*　*　*　*

Megan knew she was running late for school and it made her mad. It was Audrey's fault, of course. She was hogging the bathroom. Megan yelled through the door, "Hurry up! What's taking so long?"

"I am," came Audrey's mild voice through the door. "Honestly, Megan, you don't even wear make-up. How long do you need to be in here anyway? I've got much more to do than you."

Megan set her books down and sorted through the heap of junk on the floor of her closet, looking for her softball glove. Today was their first game of the new season. Although Miss Dadey had plenty of equipment for their squad, Megan didn't trust any glove on her hand but her own. "Ah … here it is." She punched the palm of the glove to soften it, and she ground her fist into the comfortable fold. "Perfect," she said to herself, smiling.

A glance in her dressing room mirror revealed excitement in her blue eyes. She tilted her head to one side. *Maybe a little makeup won't hurt,* she told her reflection. Then she wondered why she should bother. She never walked to school with John-Paul anymore. But Megan found blush and lipstick in a drawer and applied them anyway. She also skimmed her eyelids with a touch of lavender shadow. She had to admit she looked pretty good. Maybe Audrey was right. Maybe she should start wearing makeup more often.

Megan went into the hall and almost collided with her mother. "Good morning, Mom. You're up later than usual. Can I get you anything?" The words and cheerful attitude evaporated as she searched her mother's face.

Her mother looked rumpled and confused. She stared at her daughter and blinked as if she didn't quite recognize her.

Megan asked again, this time more slowly, "Mom, … are you okay?"

"I've lost my baby," her mother said, her voice soft and whispery.

"What baby, Mom? You don't have a baby."

"Why, yes, I do. Where's Thad? Where's my baby boy?"

Megan felt cold all of a sudden. She reached out and took her mother's arm. "Thad's eight years old, Mom. Don't you remember?"

Her mother looked even more confused. "He is? My baby is eight years old?"

"Why don't I put you back in bed for a while. Get some more rest and then when you wake up, maybe you'll remember again."

"Yes … of course … if you say so. What a silly mistake for me to make." Mrs. McCaffery followed Megan meekly down the hall to her room. Megan put her gently to bed and tucked the covers under her chin.

Megan stepped away, a cold fear clinging to her heart and mind. What was happening to her mother now? Facts from her reading rose to haunt her.

Sometimes as a tumor grows, its presses into healthy memory centers or motor areas. This pressure can manifest itself in erratic behavior or personality changes …

Megan shoved the words aside. Impossible! The X-rays had shown that her mother was practically tumor-free—that she was doing fine.

Megan dismissed the notion and chalked up her mother's temporary confusion to something else. Maybe she'd been dreaming and hadn't awakened fully before she got up. That had to be it. Megan hurried down the hall, casting out the fear with her calm, logical explanation. Her mother was fine, just fine.

* * * * *

74

The afternoon was blustery and cool. The sun kept trying to force its way through gray clouds that wanted to release rain. Megan hunched over her position on second base, resting her gloved hand on her knee. She eyed the runner at first, who kept taking a long lead. Megan watched Delsey on the pitcher's mound and thought, *What's the matter with her? Can't she see that that runner's going to try to steal second?* Megan knew that the girl was pushing her luck. If Delsey fired fast enough, Megan could tag her out.

They were down by two runs anyway. They had to start taking chances if they were going to win. Megan shivered in the cold, feeling anxious. She hadn't played very well so far and she didn't know why. She'd have to concentrate if they were going to win this game. Megan shook her head, allowing the wind to carry wisps of her hair from beneath her cap. She stared down at the dry, brittle infield grass.

The runner suddenly came at Megan, streaking toward her down the baseline. At the same moment, Delsey turned and fired the ball at Megan. The throw was wide, so Megan extended herself, stretching sideways to snag it. Her toe barely touched the base. She caught the ball as the runner slid cleat-first and slammed into Megan's ankles. The umpire yelled, "Safe!" Megan hit the ground hard and came up fighting mad.

"No way!" Megan countered. "Besides, she took me out on purpose."

The girl stood up and dusted off her uniform with a smug look on her face. Megan longed to knock it off. The girl said, "Next time, get out of my way."

"Get out of my face, you toad!" Megan shouted.

The girl spit at her feet. Megan swung. They hit the ground together, rolling and swinging. The infield swarmed with players. Megan tasted dirt and felt hands trying to force her face against the hard surface. Dust and grit filled her mouth and nose. Her balled fist connected against the girl's stomach. Megan heard the whoosh of air as the girl gasped. She went hot all over, like rockets were blowing up inside her. She couldn't stop rolling and pounding.

Suddenly strong hands tugged and pulled at her shoulders and waist. For the first time, she heard someone shouting her name, and she was separated from the other girl. Miss Dadey's voice began to penetrate her anger. "Stop it, McCaffery! Stop it this minute!"

Megan stood upright, her arms were pinned to

her sides by her coach, and she glared at her opponent. The girl's nose was bleeding and her face was streaked with dirt.

The air became cool against Megan's cheeks as her anger evaporated into the wind. All she saw was Miss Dadey's white-lipped expression and her narrowed, seething eyes. "McCaffery, you're out of the game!"

"But Miss Dadey—"

"I'll see you in my office after the game. Then we'll talk about the rest of the season. Get back to the locker room and wait for me. You're in a heap of trouble. Now move it!"

Ten

"It's about time you made an appearance!"

Megan emerged from the gym and stopped short at the sound of John-Paul's voice. He stepped forward from where he'd been leaning against the brick wall of the school. He was wearing jeans and a black sweatshirt.

She shifted her backpack and tried to step around him. "I'm not punching a time clock, you know."

He refused to let her pass. "So what did Miss Dadey say?"

"Boy, good news certainly travels fast," Megan snapped, her nerves already taut from her meeting with the coach. "Is there a TV and camera crew with you? Maybe I can make the six o'clock news."

"Just me," John-Paul answered. "Did you think you could hide in the gym forever?"

"I wasn't hiding, John-Paul. But I would like a little privacy." She sidestepped him and took off at a fast pace, anxious to put as much distance as possible between herself and the school—and anyone else who might be waiting to jump out and grill her. She'd hung around inside for as long as she could after her meeting with the coach, but seeing John-Paul meant that it hadn't been nearly long enough.

He caught up with her and fell into step beside her. "So what did she say to you?"

A lump swelled in Megan's throat. "She's making me sit the bench for the next three games and says if I have one more problem during a game, she'll suspend me from school. There, are you satisfied?" Inwardly she commanded herself not to cry.

"Why did you do it? Why did you get into a fight?"

She stopped and practically shouted at him, "Leave me alone! You're not my conscience. Go away and let me be!"

He glowered down at her, his dark eyes like glowing coals, his straight black hair catching what was left of the weak sunlight. He took her arm. "Come on."

"Where?" She tried to resist, but his grip was firm.

"We're going over to the track at the park."

"Why?" Megan asked finally.

"Because I said so."

Megan was tired of people telling her what to do, but she gave in to John-Paul. It beat going home and telling her family about being suspended for three games for fighting.

"I heard you gave her a bloody nose."

"Who?"

"The girl who slid into you."

A satisfied half-smile lifted the corner of Megan's mouth. "She bled all over the place."

"It's nothing to smile about," he told her.

"You're probably right," Megan said, still smiling.

They arrived at the park. It was deserted. A strong breeze whipped dust into whirling dirt devils on the clay track. The sky darkened and clouds rolled past in billowing gray clumps. Megan's teeth began to chatter, but John-Paul ignored her. He dropped her arm, and she rubbed where his fingers had pressed and hurt. He took her backpack and anchored it beneath his under a trash container. "In case it storms," he said.

"What are you doing?" Megan asked curiously.

"You always said you could outrun me."

"I still can," she said stubbornly.

"Then here's your chance. Prove it."

"Right now?" She blinked in surprise. She didn't know what she'd expected, but it wasn't a race.

"Yes, Megan. Right now. I'll race you for as far and as long as you can run. I'll even give you a head start. But it won't matter, because I'll beat you."

His challenge annoyed her and caused adrenaline to pump through her veins. "You'll never beat me."

"Take off," he demanded.

His insistence made her even more determined to beat him. "You're on," she said.

Megan dropped into a semi-crouch and took off. At the quarter-mile pole, she decided she'd better pace herself and slowed, glancing over her shoulder to see that he'd only just started after her. She circled the track twice, her lungs burning and her head pounding. Her breath came in gasps, and her mouth was dry, layered with dust.

The third time around, she hit her stride and the effort didn't hurt anymore. She felt the wind slap her face, and her hair streamed behind her. She heard her feet pound the hard, gritty ground. She smelled the coming rain. She lost count of how many times she circled the track. She wasn't sure where John-Paul was, either. She couldn't break her concentration to look for him. She only knew that she *had* to run. She had to rip out the hurt and anger that was eating her up inside.

Her legs, once sure and steady, began to feel weak and rubbery. Megan gritted her teeth and kept running. She felt the splat of several fat raindrops on her forehead. They were cold. She allowed herself the luxury of turning her head and was amazed to see John-Paul running to her right. She dug in with gutsy determination and forced her legs to pump harder.

By now, the rain was falling harder. It began to puddle on the track, and the splash of her sneakers forced water up her legs until she was drenched. But still she ran. Her hair was clumped in wet, ragged strands, and her vision blurred as the water streamed down her face. She stumbled and a terrible, wrenching sob ripped from her throat. Horrified, she realized that the water in her eyes was part raindrops and part tears.

Her legs faltered again and another sob escaped. She pitched forward, but John-Paul caught her. She struggled briefly, too exhausted to do more than twist feebly. She sank to her knees on the muddy track while the rain pelted her. John-Paul sank with her, his arms holding her close and hard against his chest. Unable to stop herself, she cried.

She couldn't guess how long they stayed that

way, on their knees in the middle of the track, but she cried for a long time. John-Paul rocked her gently until the terrible ache inside her was gone and she was left with a hollow, empty feeling. The rain slowed down and she began to shiver. Finally, John-Paul asked her, "Can you walk?"

She only nodded. Her attempt to stand was weak, but he helped her, wrapping his arm around her shoulders. He led her to a damp bleacher and sat her down. He sat with her, keeping her close to help stop the shivering. He said, "Do you want to talk?"

"What's to say?" Her voice was shaky. "You beat me."

He laughed, and the sound was so sweet to her that she smiled hesitantly.

"I don't know why I acted that way," she said. "I didn't mean to start crying."

"You needed to. My mother always says there's nothing like a good cry to make you feel cleaned out inside."

"It—it's not about being benched, you know. I don't really care about that. I shouldn't have been fighting."

"It's everything else, isn't it?"

She could only nod, surprised at the fresh rush

of tears that sprang from her eyes. "I don't think Mom's going to get well. She … she doesn't act right …"

A bird, searching for a meal on the newly wet ground, hopped in front of the bleacher. She watched it devour a bug. "What are we going to do, John-Paul? What am I going to do?" Her voice cracked.

He squeezed her shoulders and smoothed her hair. John-Paul spoke slowly as if he were searching for the right words. "If I were you, I'd go home and spend every single minute that I could with her. I'd pitch in and help with the wedding. I'd sit in your mom's room, on her bed every day and night. I'd just soak up all the time she has left and wallow in it like a pile of leaves. Remember how we used to do that?"

Megan nodded.

"Your dad would rake them into a heap, and we'd jump through them and bury each other in them. Well, that's how I'd act toward your mom. I'd keep all of her that I could in my mind. You know, store it up for tomorrow, for the time she goes away."

Once he said it, it made perfect sense. Of course—store up the time they had left and treasure it. Megan knew she needed to stop bucking the tide and start helping with Audrey's wedding. She'd become her mother's right hand. She'd be with her every waking moment. The solution was really very simple. Megan pulled away from John-Paul, suddenly shy and awkward. "Do you think I'll still look good in lilac?"

Water dripped off the tips of his hair and a smile lit up his face. "About as good as I'll look in a black, monkey-suit tuxedo with a lilac bowtie."

She wrinkled her nose. "You're a real sport, John-Paul, letting our sisters dress you in lilac. Are they going to give you a lilac bouquet, too?"

"Watch it. Don't go giving them any ideas." He helped her up and got their backpacks. Together they started home, soaked and exhausted. But for Megan, it was the first time in months she'd felt at peace.

Eleven

To Audrey's credit and to Megan's surprise, Audrey never once acted snooty that Megan had changed her mind and intended to be in the wedding. Audrey had simply smiled and said, "Wonderful! Mom needs to be fitted for her dress, so we'll all go to the bridal shop this Saturday and get your dress."

Megan's best reward over her change of heart had come from her mother. Her mom had reached over from her bed, clasped Megan's hand, and squeezed it warmly. A bright smile lit up her mother's face, and Megan felt heart-bursting satisfaction over having made her mother so happy.

Yvette's Bridal Salon was in the heart of historic Charleston, tucked inside an old brick building. The store's interior was elegant with its pink and white drapes and deep-rose-colored carpeting. Fancy crepe bells hung here and there, and clusters of fresh bouquets sprouted from pink porcelain vases.

The dressing rooms were large enough to hold

six people at a time. Gleaming and sparkling mirrors banked one wall. They reflected the jeweled light from a crystal chandelier that hung from the ceiling. Megan's mom sat on a pale pink sofa and sipped tea while Megan tried on the bridesmaid dress Audrey had chosen.

Megan groaned when she saw herself in the mirror. The dress was all ruffles and lace with a big hoopskirt. "I look terrible, "Megan said.

"But, Megan," Audrey reasoned, "this is a traditional wedding. I want you girls to look like Southern plantation belles. You need a full, bell-shaped skirt all the way to the floor. Please, don't be hardheaded."

"I look stupid in layers of ruffles, Audrey. It isn't me," Megan turned to the saleswoman with a pleading look.

The woman, Miss Pamela, tapped the side of her cheek with a fingernail. "She is right, you know, Audrey." Miss Pamela's voice held a hint of a French accent, which Megan suspected was faked. "Her shape is not right for ruffles and stiffness."

Megan's mother cleared her throat and fiddled with the bright scarf that covered her head. "I saw something when we came in. Perhaps that would be more appropriate."

After a quick conference, the saleswoman left and returned with a filmy satin-and-lace dress of the softest lavender. The color was breathtaking and looked stunning with Megan's fair coloring. Miss Pamela helped her into it and stepped back. "Magnificent!"

Megan stood on the pedestal in front of the mirrors and stared at herself. *Could that really be me?* She looked like something out of a magazine. The dress hung in clinging folds of satin to the floor. An intricate network of lace covered the shimmering satin, and every time she moved the satin rippled and the lace swirled. A film of lace covered her shoulders and arms all the way to her wrists. The lace rode high against her throat in front and opened in the back, exposing her neck and upper back.

"You look absolutely beautiful, Megan," Mrs. McCaffery said.

"But, Mom," Audrey protested. "The dresses have already been ordered and—"

Mrs. McCaffery looked at Audrey with a meaningful stare that made her stop mid-sentence.

Then Miss Pamela spoke up. "I don't believe that the order has gone out yet. It's not too late to change the dresses for the other girls."

Megan smiled and lifted her hair off of her shoulders. She held it high on top of her head. "I could put my hair up and wear some makeup."

Audrey smiled reluctantly. "It does look wonderful on you. With the right makeup … Rosemary could work on that for you."

They left the bridal shop with promises from Miss Pamela that all of the dresses would be ready for a final fitting by the first of March. On the ride home, Megan was silent, pondering how different she'd looked in the gown, how beautiful and transformed she'd felt. She wondered what John-Paul would think when he saw her. Her heart beat a pitty-pat rhythm at the thought.

Megan began to take serious interest in the wedding. She was actually looking forward to the wedding and to the reception, which would be held at their house under tents in the backyard. "The flowers will be blooming," Audrey explained with slightly starry eyes. "The azaleas and dogwoods and, of course, everything else will be turning green. It'll be perfect."

Megan asked, "What if it rains?"

"It wouldn't dare," Audrey declared, and somehow Megan believed her.

"What about the food?"

"It's all being catered. I'm having tea sandwiches, fresh fruit, all kinds of little hors d'oeuvres, and naturally, the wedding cake. Oh, Megan, the cake will be gorgeous! It will be three tiers high with white frosting and pink roses …" Audrey's voice trailed off and Megan shrugged, unable to see what was so enthralling about an oversized, frosted cake.

Megan helped sort through the response cards from the invitations. She noticed one in particular. The Thorndykes had accepted. That meant that Becky would be in Megan's house, in Megan's yard, flirting with John-Paul for all she was worth. Megan thoughtfully tapped the card against the table and wondered if John-Paul would even notice her with Becky around.

The final days wound down, and Mr. McCaffery grumbled about how he wasn't good for much of anything but signing checks. Audrey kissed his cheek and hugged him. "You're the father of the bride, Daddy. And you'll be the best-looking man in the ceremony."

"There's not much use for the brother of the bride either," Thad piped in.

"You'll be walking with the flower girl," Audrey told him. "That's an important job."

Thad rolled his eyes and moaned. "Lucky me."

Nothing went right at the rehearsal. The flower girl cried and refused to walk down the aisle next to Thad. Rosemary had a terrible cold and couldn't stop sneezing. John-Paul had a paper due and spent every spare minute scribbling a final draft in the back of the church pews. Mrs. McCaffery didn't feel well and had to be taken home early. The minister assured Audrey that a disastrous rehearsal made for a smooth ceremony, but Audrey looked as if she didn't believe him.

The night before the wedding, Megan and Audrey stole into their mother's room and settled on her bed. They shared hot tea, a plate of cookies, and icy cold milk. In the lamplight, without a head covering, their mother resembled a shorn lamb. Her auburn hair was no longer than an inch all over.

"It's your last night in this house as an unmarried woman, Audrey," Mrs. McCaffery said, hugging her blue fleece nightgown more tightly to her thin arms and body.

Megan added, "Yeah, tomorrow night you'll be with Brent in the Bahamas."

"Are you packed?" Mrs. McCaffery asked Audrey.

Audrey nodded. "And the suitcases are locked, too." She shot Megan a warning look. Until that moment, Megan hadn't even considered doing something silly to her sister's luggage. There would have been a time when she'd have planned it for weeks, but now …

"After the reception, Brent and I will change up here, and then Dad will drive us to the airport. Dad's the only one I trust to get us there before the plane takes off to Miami."

"Why not?" Megan asked drolly. "It's the only part he doesn't have to pay for."

Audrey ignored the remark. "Will you come along too, Mom?"

"Probably not. I'm sure the day will wear me out and I'd best not overdo it." Her disease cast a shadow over the room for a moment. "But I'll have a welcome-home dinner waiting for you two when you get back, Mrs. Coleman. How's that sound?"

"It's a deal." Audrey focused her attention on Megan. "Will you be able to hold down the fort and help Mom while I'm gone?"

"Daddy's getting a part-time housekeeper, and I can start supper when Mom doesn't feel like it. We'll be fine, Audrey."

Megan was surprised to see a film of tears over Audrey's eyes. There were tears in her mom's eyes, too. "What's the problem?" she asked her older sister.

"Nothing." Audrey twisted her engagement ring on her finger. "It's just that this is good-bye to my childhood."

Megan realized that Audrey was right. It was good-bye all right. Megan stirred on the bed, rubbing out a slight cramp in her calf muscle. "We'll always be sisters," she said. "Nothing will ever change that."

Audrey nodded solemnly. "I fought with you a lot, Megan, but I never meant any harm by it."

Megan's cheeks turned red and she felt a lump rise in her throat. "Now don't go getting sentimental on me," she said.

Audrey smiled. "Perish the thought," she said. Then she reached over and slipped her arms around Megan and drew her close. Megan hugged Audrey hard. Audrey whispered, "I love you, Meggy."

Megan loved Audrey, too. At that moment, she loved her in a way that made Megan forget all their squabbles and fights over the years.

Twelve

In the close confines of the church's dressing quarters, Megan fidgeted with her dress and hair. She was sitting in the corner, trying to stay away from the giggling bridesmaids and their clouds of hairspray and perfume.

She caught sight of herself in the mirror. Megan was surprised that the image was truly hers. A hair stylist had swept her hair into an elegant twist, leaving little curls on her forehead and cheeks. The stylist had pinned a fragrant spray of lilacs on one side and had laced tiny, violet-hued ribbons through the back. Rosemary had dusted her face with blush and powder and had accented her eyelids with pale lavender shadow. She had glossed Megan's mouth with a pale pink lipstick that shimmered when it caught the light. Megan looked better than she ever had, and she knew it. She wasn't sure if she was more nervous about the ceremony or the thought of John-Paul seeing her like this for the first time.

Megan's eyes were stinging from the aerosol sprays, so she slipped into the hallway and made her way past the photographer into the meditation chapel. The small room that adjoined the giant sanctuary was flooded with sunlight.

Megan entered the room and sighed in the stillness before she realized that she was not alone. In the very front pew was her mother. Megan approached her cautiously, careful not to disturb her. Mrs. McCaffery glanced up, caught Megan's eye, and smiled invitingly. She patted the padded pew, and Megan settled next to her. "Just catching my breath, " Mrs. McCaffery said.

"Me, too. I thought I was going to choke on hairspray." Megan was whispering but she didn't know why. They were the only ones in the room. Megan studied the ribbons of sunlight shining through the small glass window. "It's a pretty day for a wedding," she said.

"I think Audrey ordered it extra-special. The reception will be wonderful."

"Do you feel all right, Mom?" Megan asked, looking at her mother. Mrs. McCaffery looked frail, in spite of the light blue linen dress and blue satin turban on her head.

"I'm a little tired," her mother admitted. She

touched her turban. "I feel like a sultan in this thing. Does the rhinestone pin look too glittery? Audrey thought it was a nice touch."

Megan studied the sparkling pin. "It's pretty." She looked at her mother's hands, resting on her lap. They were thin and fragile. Megan saw the blue veins, the way her mother's rings hung loosely. A lump rose in Megan's throat. "Why do we cry at weddings?"

"It's a tradition."

"You won't be at my wedding, will you, Mom?" The words were out before Megan realized she'd spoken them. She shuddered slightly at what they meant.

Her mother puckered her finely shaped mouth and reached over to take Megan's hand. "I don't think so, Megan."

Her mother's honesty hit Megan like a weight, pressing tightly against her chest. She felt lightheaded. "That's why you wanted me to have a dress that was this pretty, isn't it?" She touched the rich fabric of the dress.

Her mother stared straight ahead, stroking Megan's hands in light, feathery strokes. "You're the middle child, Megan. The one who sneaked into our lives and stole our hearts completely. You wore your sister's hand-me-downs, played with your sister's discarded dolls, and never thought twice about it. You toddled off behind her, then decided to become your own person and be as different from Audrey as humanly possible. You were the one your father and I lay awake talking about into the wee hours of the night, because you were so determined to be different. And you were the one most like me."

Her mother's comment surprised Megan. She'd never thought that her parents ever gave her so much thought. Audrey had been the firstborn, and Thad was the only boy. Megan—in the middle—had always felt slighted, like she was constantly trying to catch up or make up for something. "I'm like you, Mom?"

"When I was eleven, I could climb a tree faster than a monkey, throw a ball farther than anybody my age, and get into more mischief than two kids."

"You could?" Megan could scarcely believe her ears. Her mother had always seemed so ladylike.

"It shouldn't surprise you. Where do you think you get your athletic skills? Why do you think I would never miss one of your softball games or any of Thad's Little League games?"

"I never thought about it."

"Of course, my parents were upset. They were determined I would be more of a lady. And I managed, in spite of my tomboy handicap, to grow up properly." She smiled softly, as if seeing pictures Megan couldn't share. "I lacked patience, too. Because I could do something well, I couldn't understand why another person couldn't do it just as well as I could."

Guiltily, Megan glanced down and scuffed her satin high-heeled pumps on the carpet. "I lose patience easily, don't I?"

Mrs. McCaffery didn't answer directly. Instead she concentrated on the altar in the chapel and on the brilliant spray of sunshine. When she did speak, her voice seemed to come to Megan from a long way off. "Megan, when I'm gone … when there's just you and Thad, be kind to him."

Fear gripped Megan's heart. "You're talking foolishly, Mom. It's Audrey's wedding day, and you're not going anyplace except down the aisle on the usher's arm." Fear made her words tumble out too fast.

"That's true," her mother's expression turned happy. "And speaking of going down the aisle," she said as she rose, "we'd better get back to the dressing room before Audrey comes looking for us."

Megan blinked rapidly to control the tears. She couldn't cry and spoil her makeup. Audrey would kill her. "Let's go," she said and walked with her mother from the chapel without another word.

The ceremony went perfectly. Audrey looked dazzling in her white satin-and-lace dress. Megan's best moment was when she stepped forward and took John-Paul's arm. He sucked in his breath, and his eyes grew wide when he saw her. Megan flashed him a smile. She almost floated down the aisle on his arm at the ceremony's end.

*   *   *   *   *

The photographs took forever. First, the photographer took shots of Audrey and Brent. Next he captured the bridal couple with the bride's family, then with the groom's family, then with the wedding party. The final two photos were of the bridesmaids only and the groomsmen only. Megan thought they'd never get out of the church and back to the house.

They rode to the reception in limousines. The bride and groom rode in one, both sets of parents in another, and the bridal party in two more. Megan sat between Rosemary and John-Paul. John-Paul stared out the window the whole way.

What are you thinking, John-Paul Harrison?
Megan wondered.

The car hummed, weaving its way through the Saturday afternoon traffic. Rosemary kept whispering to her escort, who laughed every once in a while.

Megan recalled seeing Becky in the pews when she walked back up the aisle following the nuptials. She'd been toward the front of the church and had been dressed in a flowered yellow dress. She'd worn a yellow hat, too, and even Megan had to admit that Becky looked sophisticated. Megan felt butterflies in her stomach as they approached the house. The limousine rolled to a stop and they got out. John-Paul extended his arm and Megan took it. They walked in silence around the side of the house, down the flagstone steps, and through newly greening grass.

Megan's mother had been right. The day was perfect. The sky was pale blue and dotted with puffy white clouds. Three blue-and-white-striped tents were placed on the sloping lawn. Inside the gazebo, an elegant wedding cake waited to be cut and served. Guests milled on the lawn. A six-piece orchestra with a harpist sent music wafting into the flowering trees.

Megan stared in amazement at the transformation that had occurred since they'd left for the church that morning. "It's beautiful," she whispered.

"Yes, it is," John-Paul agreed.

From their left, Becky Thorndyke rushed forward. She grabbed John-Paul's arm and pulled him away from Megan's side.

"I've been waiting for you, John-Paul," she said. "I'm so glad you're here. Now we can have the whole afternoon together."

Thirteen

Megan backed away and felt her cheeks grow hot.

In one smooth motion, Becky linked her arm through John-Paul's and fluttered her lashes upward. "Hi to you, too, Megan. My, it was a beautiful wedding. Audrey and Brent absolutely took my breath away."

Not far enough away, Megan thought sourly.

Becky brushed John-Paul's shoulder with the brim of her hat. Megan considered knocking it off her head, but then remembered what had happened the last time she'd lost her temper. She wasn't going to allow Becky to get on her nerves today. It was a once-in-a-lifetime day, so Megan decided to let Becky and John-Paul do whatever they wanted.

"Will you excuse me?" she said calmly. "I want to check on my mother." Megan retreated without a backward glance, hurrying up the steps to the central canopy where Audrey, Brent, and the parents of the bride and groom were seated.

She came up behind her mother, leaned down, and kissed her cheek. "Everything's wonderful, Mom. And we made it through."

Mrs. McCaffery reached up and patted Megan's arm lovingly. "So we did."

Mr. McCaffery stood up from his chair and held out his hand to Audrey. "The orchestra's playing our song, Audrey. May I have the pleasure of this dance?"

Audrey went to her father's arms. He led her out into the sunlight and onto a platform, where she gathered the intricate train of her gown onto her arm and followed his lead in a slow, leisurely waltz. Guests formed a circle around the dance floor and applauded. Megan watched the sunlight glimmer on her father's silver hair. After some minutes, Mr. McCaffery led Audrey to Brent, looking wonderful in his uniform at the edge of the crowd. The father of the bride handed over his daughter's hand to Brent. The bride and groom circled the floor alone for a few moments. Then, other members of the wedding party joined them, and finally, the guests.

"Would you like to dance with me?" Megan spun around at the invitation. John-Paul held out his hand. Megan took it, swallowing hard before they walked out onto the dance floor.

Even though she was wearing heels, Megan found that her forehead barely skimmed the bottom of his chin. She felt his arm wrap around her waist, snug and secure. She focused on the pearl buttons of his shirt. He'd loosened his lilac bowtie and had released the top button.

"Where's Becky?" Megan asked.

"I wouldn't know. And I don't care."

"It doesn't seem right that you'd walk off and leave her," Megan said.

"Would you like me to go find her?" he asked teasingly.

Her eyes drifted to his face, and she offered him a smile. "Not really."

He smiled back. "Come with me."

They stopped dancing, and he took her arm and led her across the lawn. The music and chatter of the guests faded as they walked to a secluded place in the garden. Bushes of azaleas engulfed them. A branch reached out and snagged at Megan's hair, but she loosed it and continued to follow John-Paul. He stopped in a small clearing circled by bushes.

Megan felt the tightness in her chest again. "When did you find this place?" Megan asked John-Paul. It couldn't be seen from the other side of the bushes. She'd explored the yard all her life and had never discovered it.

A mischievous glint sparkled in John-Paul's eyes. "Remember when we were little and played hide-and-seek and you could never find me?"

"You always got to home base, and I could never figure out how. Is this where you hid?"

"This is it." He reached over and touched the lilacs in her hair. "I like your hair this way." Megan felt the spray vibrate, and her knees went weak and jittery.

He took both of her hands in one of his and stared hard at her face. She brought up her face, tilted it, and looked straight into his eyes. "Are you going to kiss me, John-Paul?"

John-Paul nodded nervously.

"You could've done it many times before. Why now?" she asked softly.

"I never wanted to be in a rush."

She watched his mouth descend, watched until it blurred, and her eyelids automatically closed. When their lips met, Megan felt a melting sensation all through her, as if she were floating on a huge ocean. John-Paul kept his word. He didn't hurry.

* * * * *

Later, after Audrey and Brent had left for the airport and the guests had gone home, Megan walked on the lawn in her stocking feet. She smiled and felt warm and glowing. The grass felt tickly. She was ruining her stockings, but she didn't care.

In the grass, loose rice was scattered here and there. The air had grown colder, almost nippy. Megan circled the lawn, ignoring the workers who were taking down the tents. She remembered everyone lining up to toss rice and Thad and Billy writing "Just Married" and "Chained Forever" on the car with soap.

And she kept thinking about John-Paul's kiss. The wedding had been wonderful. But John-Paul's kiss had been the most wonderful thing she had felt in her whole life.

Megan stooped and retrieved a napkin that was fluttering on a bush. The words *Brent and Audrey* were printed on it in silver. She held it in her hands, then turned and headed toward the house. Inside, the house was quiet. Thad had gone to Billy's. Her father was on his way back from the airport.

"Mom," Megan called. Then she called again, more loudly, "Mom!"

"I'm here, honey."

Megan swung through the dining room door and entered the foyer. Her mother was sitting on one step midway up the stairs, one hand gripping the banister.

"My goodness, Mom, what are you doing sitting on the stairs?" Megan strode over to the stairs and stood below her, gazing upward.

"Hoping someone would come along and take me the rest of the way to my room."

A prickly sensation inched through Megan's body. The quiet descended like a dome. "What's wrong, Mom? Can't you walk to your room by yourself?"

A smile, brief and fluttery, graced her mother's mouth. She held out her hand and groped the empty air in front of her. "I would, baby, if I could. But it seems that I've gone quite blind."

Fourteen

"Dr. Van Avery says that the tumor's grown back," Mr. McCaffery told Megan and Thad while they ate take-out fried chicken at their dining room table. Their mother was back in the hospital again. "It's pressing against the optic nerve and that's why she can't see. But the blindness is partial. As the tumor grows, it'll shift. Kids," his voice went low. "Your mother's very ill."

"But she was doing so well!" Megan protested, jabbing the chicken with a vicious thrust of her fork.

"Not anymore."

The chicken grew cold on paper plates while Megan considered her father's words. He looked tired and worn out. The lines on his face had grown deeper over the past few days. Thad's lower lip jutted out in a pout. "I want my mother to get well and come home."

Mr. McCaffery rubbed his eyes wearily. "She's losing the battle, son."

Megan exploded out of her chair. "I don't believe it! I can't believe that those doctors are giving up on her. Well, *I'm* not. There are other doctors, other treatments. We'll find doctors who are smarter and who aren't quitters. She can't die. She just can't."

Mr. McCaffery looked at Megan with one of his strong but gentle stares. Meekly Megan sat back down, feeling small and miserable.

"There are no other treatments, Megan."

Megan's voice trembled as she asked, "What are we going to do?"

"I want to bring her home. We already have a housekeeper. Now we'll hire a nurse, and hospice will help, too. There are special caregivers who come to people's homes to help patients like your mother. With all of our help, her last days can be as comfortable and as normal as possible. Audrey and Brent live near enough that Audrey can spend time with her every day, too. I think it's best for your mother to be around her family. Can we do that?"

Last days. The words felt heavy. Thad nodded without speaking.

"Of course, we can," Megan said, poking the greasy chicken with her finger. It was useless to argue with her dad. "It's best, Dad. Best for Mom to be here with us." She felt battered inside, as if she'd been slapped by the hurricane winds that sometimes slammed into the Carolina coast. She didn't want her mother to die, but she didn't want her stuck in a hospital surrounded by strangers either. And who could say? Once she was at the house with everyone around her, she might get well. Miracles happened. Why couldn't one happen to her mother?

In April, after Easter, Mrs. McCaffery came home. She had just gotten over a long bout with pneumonia. Megan stood with Thad on the second-floor landing and watched the ambulance attendants carry their mother up the stairs on a stretcher. Her bedroom had been turned into a sort of hospital room. The big, old, four-poster bed had been removed, and a hospital bed with metal side rails stood in its place. A few pieces of medical equipment had also been placed in the room. And the dresser top was lined with pill bottles.

Thad and Megan had made a banner that hung over the bed. It said: "Welcome Home, Mom!" Megan had picked flowers from her mother's garden and set them in a vase by her bed. They'd closed the blinds to shut out the sun, but

Megan's mom asked her to please let in the sunshine. So Megan opened the curtains and blinds, allowing golden light to enter the room.

Audrey came and fussed over her mother. Megan helped her dad move his things into Audrey's old room so her mother could have privacy and comfort. That very afternoon, Mrs. Francis, the nurse, came. She was a middle-aged woman, stout and fair-haired with brown eyes and quick, sure hands. "I'll come five days a week," she told the family. "I'll arrive at seven-thirty in the morning and stay until four, when you both are home." Then she turned to Megan and Thad and said, "I'll give her the best care in the world."

"How long have you been doing this?" Megan asked. She appreciated the woman's kindness in coming to take care of her mother until she recovered.

"Ten years," Mrs. Francis said. "Ever since my son died of leukemia. Sometimes it's much easier on the families if the patient is home in familiar surroundings. That way everybody can be together."

Megan said, "We didn't bring her here to die, you know. We brought her home so she can get well. I appreciate all you're doing to help, but when she's well, we won't be needing you."

Mrs. Francis opened her mouth as if to say something. Then she stopped and gave Megan a kind smile. "Hope is the best medicine in the world, Megan. Don't ever lose it."

Confidence flooded through Megan. Now that her mom was back under her own roof and had a full-time nurse, she could get well in peace. There would be no more radiation to make her sick, no more stays in the hospital to drain her energy. With Audrey's wedding over, Megan's mom had all the time in the world to recover and get well. Megan looked forward to having her mother help her shop for summer clothes as soon as school was out.

In school, Megan carried on as if nothing was wrong. She did her work, played on the softball team, and never got into trouble. The only thing she had a hard time balancing was being around John-Paul. No matter how heavy life got, Megan couldn't forget the afternoon of the wedding when he'd kissed her in the garden. For a long time, she pretended it never happened so she could be around him without acting weird.

John-Paul was kind to her and sometimes she thought she saw him watching her with a funny look on his face, but he never mentioned the garden. After a while, she decided that he must have thought he'd made a mistake. There were days—especially when he was around Becky—that Megan thought she'd dreamed the whole fairy-tale moment. Still, it didn't stop her from secretly wanting him to kiss her again.

The one time they discussed her mother, they got into a heated argument. Walking home from school, John-Paul said, "She looks really sick to me, Megan. It can't be much longer."

"What a mean thing to say, John-Paul Harrison!" Megan stopped and planted her hands on her hips. She felt her blood pound hotly in her head. "Mom's doing great! In fact, just the other day, we played a whole game of cards and she didn't get tired or anything."

John-Paul blinked at her in the warmth of the May day. "Megan, you really can't think she's going to get well."

"Of course, she is." Megan shoved past him and hurried faster toward home.

He caught up with her and spun her around to face him. "Megan McCaffery, look at me in the eye and tell me you don't know she's dying."

Megan pushed him so hard in the center of his chest that John-Paul staggered backward. He might have fallen over had he not hit a tree beside the sidewalk. "What a mean, hateful, disgusting thing to say, John-Paul. You've got a nasty mouth! Don't you ever come around me again! Do you hear me?" She turned and ran all the way home.

Megan rushed through the door in a huff, bounded up the stairs and tore into her mother's room so fast that she startled Mrs. Francis, who was reading in a nearby chair. The older woman asked, "Why, child, … what's the matter?"

"How's Mom?"

"She's resting."

The cold, tight knot of fear loosened in Megan's stomach. "Good. I–I was just checking."

Mrs. Francis said nothing. Megan left the room. She could hardly stand to look at her mother's thin and wasted body on the bed.

* * * * *

Audrey asked her father, sister, and brother to dinner. Megan, Thad, and Mr. McCaffery crowded around the table in Audrey and Brent's small apartment. Audrey told them the situation was temporary until Brent graduated and joined the Army. Thad glanced nervously at his plate, and looked at Megan. "Are you going to eat this stuff?" he asked her.

"We can't be rude," Megan whispered. "Just take small bites and drink plenty of water."

But it wasn't food that Audrey was eager to share. "Goodness," Mr. McCaffery said. "You look like the cat that ate the canary, Audrey. What do you want to tell us?"

Audrey's face lit up into a huge smile. She reached over and took her husband's hand. "Brent and I are going to have a baby," she said, beaming. "By next spring, you'll be an aunt and an uncle," she told Megan and Thad. "And, Dad, you'll be a grandfather."

Megan looked at Audrey carefully. She didn't *look* any different. It didn't seem possible that a baby was growing inside her sister.

Mr. McCaffery asked, "Have you told your mother?"

Audrey said, "I'm going by tomorrow to give her the news."

It'll give Mom something to look forward to, Megan thought.

Thad leaned over and whispered, "That poor baby's going to have to grow up eating Audrey's cooking."

Megan whispered back, "Scary, isn't it?"

* * * * *

Megan stared out the window of her class-room. The problem with the last week of school was that there was nothing to do but you had to go to classes anyway. She played with her pencil and thought about the summer that stretched in front of her. Next week she could sleep in late, go to the pool, go shopping, go skating, play ball. Too bad she and John-Paul weren't on speaking terms. She missed him. But she still hadn't forgiven him for the things he'd said about her mother that afternoon.

Megan sighed and lowered her chin to rest on her palm, braced by her elbow on her desk. The door of the classroom opened. Even before the boy approached the teacher's desk, instinct warned Megan that he was a runner from the principal's office with a message for her. She raised herself slowly and went clammy cold.

Like slow-motion scenes in a movie, her teacher, Miss Judd, looked up and said, "Megan McCaffery, you have a message. Please go to the office."

Megan never even bothered to pick up her books. She left her purse, her lunch—everything. She didn't go to the office, either. She ran, instead, down the hall to the outside door. She opened it quickly and raced into the sunshine. Her hair flew behind her in a stream, and her legs pumped hard all the way home.

Fifteen

Mr. McCaffery's car was in the driveway. A taxi was pulling away. Thad must have been sent for, too. Megan saw Audrey's car half-rammed onto the lawn, the door still open, as if she'd been in too big of a hurry to close it. Fear lodged into Megan's mouth. She slammed through the front door and took the stairs two at a time.

She hurtled into her mother's bedroom and ground to a halt at the sight of the rest of her family hovering around her mother's bed. The atmosphere was hushed, tense. On the bed, her mother struggled to breathe, the air rattling in her lungs, sounding desperate and trapped.

"What's wrong?" Megan asked.

Mrs. Francis crossed the room and took Megan's hand. "Her breathing became labored, so I thought it best to call you all home at once."

Megan's fingers went numb and cold, and cramps formed in her stomach. Mrs. Francis led her toward the bed. Her legs felt heavy, as if she could hardly lift them. Her mother looked small against the pillows. Her paper-thin skin was ashen in color. Her breathing turned light and rapid.

"Can't you do something?" Megan begged Mrs. Francis, clenching and unclenching her fists. "You're a nurse. Can't you *do* anything?" Tears flowed down her cheeks.

Mrs. Francis stroked Megan's arm. "There's nothing anyone can do."

Megan shifted her tearful gaze to the faces of her family. Thad's expression was wide-eyed, scared, and pale. Audrey's face was tear-streaked. Her father looked grim. Megan took a step backward, as if the weight of their combined grief had shoved against her. The pain inside her was unbearable. She wanted to scream and fight against the force that was stealing her mother's life.

Audrey began to mumble, to plead with their mother to stay with them. Megan fought down her own pain. She lifted her trembling chin and reached out for Thad. Her mother's words came back to her from the day of the wedding.

"Be kind to Thad ..."

"You won't be at my wedding, will, you, Mom?"

"I don't think so, Megan ... Megan, when I'm gone ... when there's just you and Thad, be kind to him."

Thad huddled close to Megan, his thin shoulders hunched and tense. Megan patted his hair, and when he turned his pleading eyes to meet hers, she whispered, "It's all right, Thad. We'll be all right." She was all her brother had now, and she must be strong for him. She willed her tears to stop. She wiped her cheeks and nose. *For Thad's sake*, she thought, *I will be strong*.

Life let go of Adele McCaffery. Life released her gently like a dandelion releases its cap of milk-white fuzz into the wind. Megan marveled over how simply, how quickly and quietly death came. One moment, Mom was breathing, and the next moment, she wasn't. One moment, her spirit was alive in her body, and then it was gone.

Megan had imagined death as horrible, agonizing. But for her mother, death brought nothing but peace. It was like crossing over a barrier. On one side of the barrier, there was life. On the other side, there was death. As her mother crossed the barrier, Megan felt numb inside.

The sweet scent of gardenias permeated the darkened quiet of the room. The only sound was

Megan watched with fascination as a bird darted from a tree branch and toward the sky. The bird flapped it invisible draft lifted it, billowing journey upward, the bird soar freely toward the sun. Ar mingled with its son Megan's crying.

heat of early summer into breeze blew in, too, whispering promises, as summer breezes often do. Above Megan, a bright blue sky spread far and wide.

Megan filled her lungs with the smells of summer—the aromas of freshly mowed grass, of summer flowers, of rich soil. Everything inside was different. The five parts of her family had been cut into fourths. But everything outside was the same. The earth turned, the sun shone, the flowers bloomed. Life—and death—went on. Her throat ached with the tears she wanted to shed.

mocking-
flew upward
s wings until an
g its feathers. In its
ed and glided, drifting
d as it flew, it sang. And
g was the gentle sound of

Epilogue

"I'm glad you're back, Megan. I missed you."

John-Paul's honesty caught Megan off guard. With his fingers laced through hers and the colors of spring all around them, Megan and John-Paul drifted across the lawn toward the gazebo.

"I'm glad to be home." She gazed around. Had it only been a year since the wedding and reception? Was it only last spring that canopies and guests had filled their lawn? Only a year since her dad had danced with Audrey while her mother watched? Only a year ago that John-Paul had kissed her in the privacy of the shimmering garden?

"So tell me about the baby," John-Paul interrupted her thoughts. "How are Audrey and Brent doing?"

Megan thought about the phone call, the call the week before announcing that the birth was near. The whole family took a plane to Fort Bragg where Brent was stationed. Megan remembered the visit to Audrey's new house, and the trips to the hospital to gaze through a glass partition at the tiny, pink-wrapped bundle. How different these trips to the hospital had been from the trips to her mother's hospital room.

"They named her Joyce Adele Coleman. I don't think I've ever seen anything so small and so pretty, John-Paul."

"Did you take pictures?"

"Hundreds." Megan said, laughing. "Dad took them to be developed this morning on his way to the office, so I'll be able to show her off in a couple of days."

"I heard the girls talking at school. I think they're jealous, you being an aunt and all."

"Becky Thorndyke, too?" Megan asked with an arch of her brow.

John-Paul's black eyes crinkled at the corners. "Becky, too."

"Good. Let her talk."

John-Paul settled beside Megan on the cool surface of the cement bench inside the gazebo. He put his arms around her shoulders.

"I got to hold the baby. Oh, John-Paul. She's like nothing I've ever seen before! She has so much hair! It's reddish and thick and so soft!"

John-Paul brushed his thumb against Megan's hair. "Who does she look like?"

"A lot like Mom. I wish Mom could see her."

"I'll bet she can."

"That's what Audrey said, too," Megan rested her head on John-Paul's shoulder. "She looks like all of us, you know. Looking at her, I saw my great-grandmother—"

"The one who burned the farm?"

"Yes. And I could see Mom. And Audrey. And Brent. I even saw myself—a little." She pulled away and peered shyly into his eyes. "Does that sound crazy?"

"No."

"Somehow families go on and on, don't they?" Megan said. "And it doesn't matter what happens— wars and sickness—we just keep going on and on." She pushed a stray strand hair behind her ear. "I still miss Mom, John-Paul."

"I don't think you'll ever stop missing her. I know I missed my dad when he and Mom got divorced and he moved away."

"But you can still see him, talk to him. I can't." Megan fell silent.

"Oh, I almost forgot," John-Paul said with a smile, calling her away from the dark emotions. "I picked this for you." He reached into the pocket of his shirt and pulled out a rosebud. "It's the first one on the bushes. It's going to be a lilac color. Pretty, huh?"

She took it gently and cradled it in her palm, admiring its unusual color. "Show me the bush it came from," she urged. "I want to watch for it to bloom so I can cut the roses and take them to Mom's grave this summer."

He took the bud and slipped it behind her ear, nestling it near her temple, securing it in her hair. He asked, "Did I ever tell you how much I like flowers in your hair?"

She blushed, remembering. "Yes, once."

He cupped her chin in his hand and brushed his lips over her ears ever so lightly. "Well, please let me tell you again." Then he kissed her. And Megan hoped the kiss would last forever.

Author's Note

For further information about support groups for those who have lost a child or sibling, contact

The Compassionate Friends, Inc.
P.O. Box 3696
Oak Brook, IL
60522-3696
Toll-free: (877) 969-0010
Fax: (630) 990-0246
E-mail: nationaloffice@compassionatefriends.org
Web site: www.compassionatefriends.org

The mission of The Compassionate Friends
is to assist families toward the positive resolution
of grief following the death of a child
of any age and to provide information to
help others be supportive.

About the Author

LURLENE McDANIEL lives in Chattanooga, Tennessee, and is a favorite author of young people all over the country. Her best-selling books about kids overcoming problems such as cancer, diabetes, and the death of a parent or sibling draw a wide response from her readers. Lurlene says that the best compliment she can receive is having a reader tell her, "Your story was so interesting that I couldn't put it down!" To Lurlene, the most important thing is writing an uplifting story that helps the reader look at life from a different perspective.

Six Months to Live, the first of the four-book series about cancer survivor Dawn Rochelle, was placed in a time capsule at the Library of Congress in Washington, D.C. The capsule is scheduled to be opened in the year 2089.

Other Darby Creek Publishing books by Lurlene McDaniel include *If I Should Die Before I Wake, A Horse for Mandy, My Secret Boyfriend,* and *Why Did She Have to Die?*

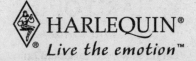